eightball

elizabeth geoghegan

E E Geoghegan

sfwp.com

The story "Cricket Boy" first appeared in *The Cream City Review* and in *Lotus-eater*. The stories "Tree Boy" and "The Violet Hour" first appeared in *Natural Disasters: Stories*.

Library of Congress Cataloging-in-Publication Data

Names: Geoghegan, Elizabeth, author.
Title: Eightball / Elizabeth Geoghegan.
Description: Santa Fe, NM : SFWP, [2019]
Identifiers: LCCN 2018040422| ISBN 9781939650955 (pbk. : alk. paper) |
    ISBN 9781939650979 (mobi) | ISBN 9781939650986 (epub)
Classification: LCC PS3607.E634 A6 2019 | DDC 813/.6—dc23
LC record available at https://lccn.loc.gov/2018040422

Cover photo: Jeannette Montgomery Barron

Published by SFWP
369 Montezuma Ave. #350
Santa Fe, NM 87501
(505) 428-9045
www.sfwp.com

In memory of my brother GMG

Table of Contents

Tree Boy

Tree Boy shows up late for class. Tight white T-shirt and steel-toe boots, his work pants washed soft and stained with tree gum. I have seen him wield a chainsaw and I have heard him go on about early photography. Talbot. Cartier-Bresson. He tells me about the places he's lived, but I can only envision him near the Pacific. A life on the Olympic Peninsula. The scarred legacy of logging trucks and poverty.

Tree Boy is both the darling and the rogue of the graduate program. A scholarship brought him to the school. Necessity makes him work on the grounds. Because he is so gifted—so clearly without need of a mentor—the faculty never lets him forget it. Offhanded comments about his worker status on campus: Tree Boy cutting down university limbs and using the take for art supplies. With their fancy pedigrees from the other coast, it's as if he embodies what they loathe most about this town so far north and west that they may as well be in Alaska. But when it is time to dole out teaching appointments or awards, they always give him the nod.

Tree Boy rents an attic near the edge of Lake Union, his windows facing west, facing home. I drop him off. He doesn't invite me in. But he begins to sit beside me in class. Or wait for me, hanging in the doorway of my studio, holding a paper cup of espresso, a crumpled brown bag full of peaches. He claims he doesn't take pictures anymore, that a photograph can never live up to the real thing. But when I show him the prints from the year I lived in Rome, he says he'd like to have one.

Tree Boy wanders into my studio late one evening. He pulls a pencil from behind his ear and absentmindedly runs it through his cropped hair. From scalp to nape and back again. He tells me he came to see my work, then stares at my photographs in silence. As he moves from shot to shot, I feel naked beneath his gaze. And I am. I've been making a series of self-portraits—close-ups of my body—so close that the landscape of skin is often unrecognizable. The crease of an elbow. The blurred edge of my inner thigh. Still, I know that he can tell the difference. Without asking, he removes a contact sheet from the wall and sits down in my chair holding 36 versions of my left breast in his hand. He looks up and tells me my photos are childish.

Then he asks me if I want to get a beer.

Seattle feels benign after Chicago. Too green and too pretty. Too sedate. There is a sinister side, but it's camouflaged behind the blooming wisteria, the innocuous bungalows built on its hills. Like Mt. Rainier, I only catch glimpses of it. Endless misty months and so many bodies of water—a wrong turn and I find myself on a long bridge, bearing it out until I can turn back on the other shore. My internal compass useless. No single lake to define east, almost as if there is no east. No light rising at dawn, only the occasional flash of color, fog lifting late on a summer evening and the ache of an overdue sunset disappearing into the Sound.

For nearly a semester I watched him trimming trees or dragging brush and loading it into his battered pickup, the white paint worn away and smooth patches of primer exposed. For months I longed to be one of those branches. To have him pull me toward him and cut me free. To feel myself falling and falling. To be the branch he sculpted into a seductive shape and placed in the gallery for everyone to see. Except Tree Boy always destroys his installations. He creates exquisite objects, then burns them to ashes, never documenting any of it, only coming round at the end of the exhibit to sweep the remains into a metal dustpan.

As we cut across the quad, he describes forest fires on the peninsula when he was growing up. I ask him if this is the reason he burns his work.

"No," he says, looking at me as if I'm stupid. "But it always ends in flames."

Before he torches it, I sneak into the gallery and photograph his most recent installation. Careful couplets etched into pine. I smooth my hand over the wood, feeling the letters as if they were veins in his lean arm. I think about the eventuality of fire, his work returning to the land as ashes beneath the suffocating ceiling of a northwest sky. Later, I tell him that he should write, and he gives me a half-hour lecture on the futility of words. The next day he brings me a copy of Berger's *Ways of Seeing*, the binding splintered, the pages warped with damp. Flipping through it, I see his perfect penmanship, initials and phone numbers lining the inside back cover. I stare at the list wondering who the people are. Mostly, I wonder how many of them are women.

Every so often he calls and asks me to look up a number. I insist on returning the book, but he refuses to take it back. He tells me that he has already read it, that he has no use for it.

I keep it like a reliquary beside my bed.

I look for answers buried in the chapters of Berger.

I commit the phone list to memory.

Even my dog has a crush on Tree Boy—she's as shameless as an undergrad. When I bring her to school she whines and cries, pawing insistently at my door. I let her out and she wanders down the hallway, circles in front of his studio, curling into position and wrapping her tail around her. I tempt her with treats, but nothing works. I give up and go into the darkroom, lose myself in the bulb's red glow, the comforting smell of chemicals. I linger until everyone leaves in search of dinner or cigarettes, and then I develop the roll of Tree Boy's work, watching the silvery images appear in the rush of water. I hide the prints in a folder and label it "kindling."

It goes on like this for weeks. I stop listening to music so I can hear my gate squeak open when he comes by. We cook late-night meals and eat sitting on the floor. He sketches me by candlelight. We drink bourbon, neat. When we are alone, he never touches me. But when colleagues or professors are watching, he will trace small, slow circles with his fingers on the inside of my wrist or stop midsentence to brush the hair back from my eyes.

One night he talks about the women he's slept with. How he touched them. And how he wanted to. Almost whispering, he tells me about his old girlfriend. How he loved to give her a bath, sitting on the cool tiles beside the tub, rinsing warm water through her hair. How after she kicked him out he ran barefoot in the Cascades until his feet were so raw and bloody that he crawled two hours back to his truck, passing hikers and mountain bikers and family picnics.

He says, "Seattle will only ever be about her."

Tree Boy tells me I will never make a really great photograph because I've never done without. I want to think he's mistaken. Part of me worries he's right. He makes a point of mentioning my bourgeois upbringing, the shrinks and family vacations, the private schools.

"I've always worked," I say. "It's not that simple."

He looks at me and smiles, in a way.

I try harder to show him who I really am. I tell him about my lovers in Chicago. The bass player, the bike messenger, the architect. I tell him what pleases me—that if a man touches my neck, just so, I will come. I tell him I like to get fucked from behind, preferring not to see faces unless I'm in love. I tell him too much and convince myself I haven't told him enough. I tell him about my first camera, a Brownie. I tell him my favorite tree, the magnolia. My favorite saint,

Lucia, the tender image of her eyeballs plucked out and placed on a plate before her.

And I tell him about long, sticky days passed at the stables. Peeling off my clothes and swimming my horse into the lake, sliding off his glossy back and being pulled by his tail through green water. And I tell him about the day he was castrated. How they left his testicles to scorch in the pasture and how—even at nine—I was compelled to photograph them as each day passed. Lumps of skin and blood shriveling in the August sun.

The telephone wakes me just before dawn. Tree Boy calling for a phone number. He softly says the initials, not offering anything more. I resist reciting the number even though I know it by heart. I put the phone down on my pillow, pretend to fumble and look, before reading out the country code for Italy, the long string of numbers beside it.

I am the branch after all. The willow that bends and bends.

But Tree Boy wants to snap me in two.

I keen my ear for the sound of his chainsaw when I'm at school. I search the parking lot. His truck isn't there. For seven days he is missing from campus. My dog keeps her vigil in front of his studio. I call all the Seattle numbers from the back of Berger. I listen closely to the sound of each woman's voice before I hang up. I contemplate dialing the number in Italy. I carry *Ways of Seeing* out to the grill instead. I soak the cover with lighter fluid, toss in a match, and martyr it like San Lorenzo, watching it burn as if waiting for the book to sit up and confront me.

In the morning, there are only ashes and gray clumps of charcoal that I poke through the grate with a stick. I switch format and continue photographing my body. I slice the images into pieces and reconfigure them, trying to turn myself into someone else.

And then there he is, lying in my hammock, my dog stretched across his chest. I don't want him to hear how happy I am to see him.

"Tree Boy, "I say, throwing a guilty glance at the Weber.

"I missed you," he says.

But when I look back, he is stroking the dog.

We climb into his truck. He turns the key in the ignition, then shuts it off, leans close, and looks at me for a long time. Just when I think he is finally going to kiss me, he reaches over and locks my door. He starts the motor again and shifts into gear, waiting until we get to the end of the block before turning on the lights. One beam weaker than the other, peering down the deserted street.

We cross a bridge, then another, heading out of the city. Trees thicken along the roadway. When he reaches to downshift, his hand brushes my leg.

"Listen," he says.

And I do listen. Only I'm listening the way I listen to the songs on a CD that precede the one I really want to hear.

He tells me about the painter he fell in love with, not for her brushstroke—which was brilliant—but for her soft Kentucky lilt with long, honeyed pauses, her penchant for the term "daddy." How he cheated on his girlfriend of seven years to pursue her. How it all began. And how it ended. How the painter was sleeping with his favorite professor, and how she followed that same professor on a Fulbright to Italy.

But by then it was too late. His girlfriend had tossed everything he ever cherished onto the driveway in the rain. For weeks she backed her car over his possessions, over his portfolio, and even over the photos he had taken of her. Ruined drawings catching on fence posts. Crumpled slides collecting with the mud and the trash along the curbs and in the drains. How what remained was eventually ground into the pavement or vanquished by moss, fecund green tendrils reclaiming the memory of who he used to be.

"So you were in Italy," I say.

Tree Boy drums his fingers on the steering wheel, and the lame headlight blinks out as if in response.

Sharp curves in the dark. Air forcing its way through the window and rattling the glass, the hermetic strip flapping against the door. For a moment, the trees open up and, even at night, I can see that the hillside has been devastated with logging. Only the stumps left behind, forlorn as headstones, amidst the furrow of tire tracks.

He pulls onto a dirt road. Scrub and branches drag against the underside of the pickup as we bump slowly along. I watch his hands, opening and closing around the wheel. He kills the engine and we roll to a stop.

He gets out and shuts the door. My dog leaps out of the back, and they both disappear in the darkness. Traitor, I think. I lift up the lock and feel for the handle. It comes off in my hand. I stare at it for a second, then put it on the dash and roll down my window. Twigs crunch underneath his boots as he comes around to my side. He opens the door and I hop down, nearly falling into his arms. Warm air and the feel of his hands. The smell of damp earth and fresh laundry—the smell of him.

Rocks ping, scattering, as we walk further and further, into the trees. The dog's collar jingles as she trots on ahead. A bird lifts from its perch in the darkness, limbs rustling. When we come out of the woods, the low red moon shimmers on the lake. I remember reading somewhere that seeing the moon's reflection on water has long been considered a cure for hysteria. I almost laugh. But now I want him more than ever.

Each detail of his betrayal only made me desire him more. I heard it as a kind of confession—him realizing that he had gotten it all wrong. Like he'd adjusted the aperture to finally put me in focus. And I don't care where he's been. Whether it was Italy or nowhere. And I don't care who or how many he's fucked if it means that now I am in the center of the frame.

The air is full of the promise of heat. His fingers move lightly across my collarbone, grazing my throat. I close my eyes. I don't want to see anything. I only want it not to stop.

It stops.

My eyes flutter open and he is already wading into the lake, his jeans soaked up to the knee. He gently takes my hand and coaxes me into the water beside him, then vanishes. He reemerges further out, floating on his back in the dark water—only I am the one who is drifting. Tall trees and a pomegranate moon. But I want the fruit pried open. Wet red seeds juicing my mouth.

Finally, he swims toward me and leads me back to shore.

I am almost surprised when he lays me down. I unbutton my shirt and he runs his callused palm over the curve of my ribs. He is neither cautious nor rough—almost clinical—as if I am timber he is inspecting for flaws. He unzips my jeans, peeling them down over my hips and resting his wet face against the flat of my belly. I can feel the stubble of his newly shaved head, the droplets of water against my skin. He circles my navel with his tongue, then lower, stopping only to guide my underwear down over my legs.

I want nothing more than the feel of him inside me.

But first I want him to kiss me, soft and slow and for a long time.

He tugs off his wet shirt and drops it. His stomach is taut, his chest bare and smooth, a tattoo of the Madonna over his heart. The ink's gone green and her face is wet with tears. I sit up and reach for him, but he takes both my wrists, clenching them in one of his hands. His body is so beautiful that I suddenly feel self-conscious. I have photographed my labia and hung the image on white walls for everyone to see; I have never felt quite so exposed.

It doesn't startle me when he pushes me down.

Or when he moves and, still holding my wrists, puts his knees on either side of my shoulders and hovers above me.

He unfastens his belt, the buckle nearly cracking me in the face.

And it's not that I don't want to.

It's that he has never kissed me.

That I can't bring myself to ask him to.

I take him in my mouth and I remember how slowly his book seemed to burn. The way the pages silently furled and went black. Sparks flaring in the wind and floating around me. Bits of char and ash falling at my feet.

As if this is all too intimate, Tree Boy loosens his grip from my wrists, moves his leg away from my side, and lifts me up toward him, rolling me over. Rocks cut into my knees and my palms slip in the mud.

And this is not how I wanted it: Tree Boy's hands parting me as branches. Tree Boy's wet jeans sawing the backs of my thighs.

I am the bough that grew too full and needs to be cut back.

I am shade where there should be light.

The Violet Hour

The summer Violet met Billy, he'd been sleeping on a futon under a tree in a backyard on the south end of town, while keeping all of his possessions in a storage locker on the north end of town. When he invited her to a party—at his place, or so she had thought—she quickly discovered the demarcation line of his room consisted of small glass lanterns dangling from the branches of a giant sycamore, and as they sat beneath its canopy of leaves, tiny candle flames dwindling like fireflies captured in so many jars, he had pulled her closer.

"Since you asked me out, I don't know what the pace is supposed to be," Billy said.

Violet had not asked Billy on a date. But she had called—to thank him.

Racing along the Diagonal toward Boulder, she'd hit a pothole and gotten a flat. She'd been standing on the side of the road longer than she cared to admit when Billy cycled up beside her, a vision in Spandex, all that tight bike gear leaving nothing to the imagination as he bent to the task of finding the jack and hoisting the spare out of the back of her car.

His brown eyes had crinkled up at the edges when she'd asked for his number, those same brown eyes he had trained on her that night. Over his shoulder, the hostess stood near the barbeque. She was uncertain of Billy's relationship to her, but the woman had studiously avoided Violet the entire evening while somehow making her every move feel observed.

She asked Billy what the pace would be if he'd done the asking out.

"Breakneck," he said.

"Well, then."

And before she knew it, she found herself putting down roots for a man whose idea of a commitment was a season pass at Vail. She convinced herself she would have stayed in Boulder and bought the house anyway, even though she knew it was Billy's dream house—not hers—tucked so far up Left Hand Canyon that days could go by seeing only deer, statue-like outside her window, or the glint of sunlight off her neighbor's fender as his pickup rattled past. And then there was the commute to her job.

There had always been question marks about Violet's relationship with Billy. She spent too much time trying to prove she was down to earth when anyone who knew Violet knew she wasn't. Billy included. But most of the time they had worked. Until he challenged her to join him on a trek along the Silk Road. But she'd anted up, quickly organizing a leave of absence from work, making arrangements with Jane to dog-sit, and subletting her house to a visiting academic. She had even caved about carrying a backpack, insisting she was ready to give up modern conveniences.

Violet wanted to be that kind of woman. The kind who roughed it across rugged terrain through countries whose names were impossible to spell and whose borders were as slippery as the dictators ruling them. She wanted that ineffable quality—the ability to look good in the morning before coffee or mascara. She relinquished the meager hope that she would find a decent hair salon in Kashgar or Varanasi or anywhere else along the route. Billy had teased her mercilessly when she made the mistake of mentioning it.

What did he expect, anyway? One day he complained she was too high maintenance. The next, he encouraged her to buy a fancy Italian espresso machine, a new SUV. And it wasn't as if he ever did without. He may have favored worn T-shirts or tattered fleece pullovers made from recycled plastic bottles, but he always had all the latest gear. Without wanting to admit it, she had begun to see that he was the kind of guy who would spend six grand on a mountain bike but stiff the waitress on a breakfast burrito. Sometimes she didn't like Billy at all. But it didn't matter if she liked him. She loved him.

And he was easy to love; half the time he wasn't even there. While she finished her MBA and worked raising funds for the museum, Billy was mostly "in the field." And he actually used that expression. It was true, she enjoyed opening *The Times* and *Outside* and seeing his photographs, but she missed him when he went on his sojourns. So, after he returned from what seemed like a particularly long stint in Tajikistan, she recounted her plans to buy a house and asked him to move in with her. She had phrased it in his language.

"You need a base camp," she said.

And he agreed.

She was eager to take him off the market. Boulder was populated with Billy's ex-girlfriends. Countless women claimed to have dated him. Few had managed to hang on to him for long. He'd sign on for a gig somewhere abroad or create some reason he absolutely had to visit the Galapagos or Nepal, then ask the woman of the moment to watch Kit, his yellow Lab. Of course, they'd all comply. Sometimes he'd call them, sometimes he'd even send small gifts wrapped in bits of newsprint with Arabic or Asian script.

Sooner or later, though, the email would always arrive, telling the woman he really appreciated the dog sitting but realized it was wrong for him to expect her to wait. He never said he didn't love her. And he never said he'd met someone else. Just that he couldn't give her what she deserved. It was always the same email. His exes had a sense of humor, anyway, joking that he kept a draft in a folder on Yahoo so he could pop into whatever excuse for an Internet café he could find, in whichever third world backwater he had traveled to, and not have to pay by the minute for the time it would take to compose the missive. Or dismissive, as it were. Still, they all continued to carry the proverbial torch, even though none could deny that when it came to Violet, Billy seemed different.

Whenever she could, Violet avoided the Billy Posse—Kelly, Caitlin, Lani, and Mel. Once, she had bumped into them at a brewpub in town. Kelly cornered her in the line outside the women's restroom.

"He always comes back to you," Kelly said. Her voice had that bright intensity common amongst world-class athletes, idealists, and vegans.

"He always comes back to Kit," Violet corrected.

Kelly was the perfect Boulder woman, a professional rock climber with zero body fat, shiny blonde hair, and a trust fund. Still worse, she was actually nice. And Billy made sure to remind Violet that Kelly volunteered, not just with Rocky Mountain Rescue, but with weekly trips to mentor children whose parents had been incarcerated. Billy had met Kelly when he'd been hired to photograph her on some impossibly technical climb near Ouray for Rock and Ice. The two spent the rest of the winter backcountry skiing and ice-climbing together in the San Juans. His portfolio was crowded with images of Kelly effortlessly hanging from her fingertips in canyons and gorges. Shots of her managing to look thin even when bundled in outdoor gear skinning up a mountain or telemarking down it. But even Kelly hadn't lasted.

The months had gone by and Violet began to relax, not just about Kelly but about all of them, and even about Billy. The sense of panic that welled up in her when she received his emails dissipated. And lo it came to pass, as they approached the end of their second year together, Billy proffered the Silk Road idea. He had made it sound easy, enticing her with a few weeks "to chill" in Southeast Asia before making their way up to China when the weather improved along the route. Violet told Jane she thought the trip would do her good.

"Lie to yourself," her friend had said, "but not to me."

Later, she sent Billy an email admitting she was worried some of the countries sounded dangerous.

"Figure it out," he wrote back, "and let me know when you can be in Bangkok."

She liked traveling, but the word "travel" evoked images of relaxing on a beach in Eleuthera or visiting the Tate Modern in London, then going out for sushi afterward. Not getting dysentery or sleeping on the floor of a yurt in one of the Stans. She had never understood how hiking could be considered a holiday. And while it was true she'd ended up in out West, Boulder wasn't the hippie town it had once been. These days, you could even buy a Marc Jacobs bag on the Pearl Street mall. She adored the mountains as much as the next person, but it had always been enough just to look at them.

While she packed up her things and made arrangements for her departure, Billy sent updates from Colombo and Jakarta. One night he called.

"Dude," he told her, "you're so gonna love it."

"I miss you," she said.

"Do you really think Jane should watch Kit? Maybe Kelly should do it."

"No," Violet said. "Not Kelly."

"But Kit really loves Kelly."

She assured him Jane could handle the dog, and he instructed her to take a bus into the city from the airport. They both knew she would take a taxi. She hung up the phone, opened her laptop, and immediately found a five-star hotel in Bangkok. At least they would spend the first few days in style, she thought. It would be her treat. She emailed him her flight confirmation and the address of the hotel. She didn't allow herself to consider what the months ahead would bring.

When she arrived on Christmas, Billy wasn't at the Shangri-La, but she was so exhausted from the long journey by way of San Francisco and Tokyo that she showered, slipped into the glorious robe hanging beside the bath, shook the Dendrobium orchids from her pillow, and crawled between the 500-thread count sheets, falling fast asleep. Hours later, she woke and all was darkness. In the distance, high-rises and boats shimmered along the Chao Phraya River, the lights of the city sprawling in every direction beneath the tall windows of her room. She had never been to Asia and had no idea what to expect of Bangkok. The cab from the airport had been slow, weaving in and out of congested lanes of traffic, but she had mostly nodded off in the backseat, barely noting anything other than the opulent lobby.

She dug her cell phone out of her bag, but it didn't receive a signal. She picked up the phone beside the bed and dialed Billy's number, but it only rang and never rolled over to voice mail. He rarely had his phone turned on, much less kept it charged. She was dismayed, just the same. The hotel was gorgeous, but she couldn't believe there was no way to check email. She considered going out but thought better of it, calling room service and ordering dinner instead.

It's no big deal, she thought. Probably he'd bought the cheapest ticket available and would show up in the middle of the night. Or maybe his plane had been delayed. It was the holidays, after all. She tried to remember where he was flying in from. Kuala Lumpur? Or was he still in Indonesia? Hadn't he been doing a story somewhere on Java? Billy's constant trips had long since blurred together, and the twenty-six hour transit time had wiped her out. She had written it all down somewhere but couldn't recall exactly where she'd put her journal. She glanced at her backpack—a dark lump in the corner and an affront to the elegance of the hotel. She hated it already. No good could come of it.

She remembered the only time she and Billy had ever taken a trip together. She thought about his confidence—his competence, really— in all things. She had joined him on a job in Italy, meeting him for what should have been a gorgeous drive along the Amalfi Coast, but there had been delays, one snafu after another, and they'd ended up in a rickety rental car with a broken windshield wiper late on a stormy afternoon. When the rain came it felt like an assault. There was literally no turning back. Not on that road.

Violet, closer to the proverbial edge than usual, had clutched the dashboard, averting her eyes from the rocks sheering away from the car toward the sea, her stomach lurching with each hairpin curve. Billy slowed and turned on the hazards, asking her to find his camera, tucked in its case and propped between her feet next to her handbag. She fumbled around, extracting his Leica and removing the lens cap. She had assumed he wanted her to try to get a shot.

"Hold the wheel," he said.

"No, Billy," she said. "No way."

There were barely twenty meters before the next sharp curve.

"Just keep it straight."

Of course, she had acquiesced, leaning over to grasp the steering wheel while Billy somehow leaned out of the driver's side window and managed to make a photo capturing all of it—the pounding rain, the headlights of the oncoming cars, picturesque Positano in the distance, the cliff edge lapsing into the endless blue that threatened to swallow them. Later, the image landed on the cover of National Geographic for an article about the world's most dangerous roads. That had been the hook. Billy's ability to turn a hardship into a thing of beauty, crystalizing it in a single image made at precisely the right moment. Plenty of people can point and shoot. Few are able to gaze through the lens and truly see.

She had been ill and anxious for days after that drive and Billy hadn't so much as broken a sweat. Violet knew how to work a boardroom, how to entertain. She was at ease dining with wealthy benefactors, always ending the evening with a check in hand. Hers was a man-made world and the only one she'd ever been comfortable in. Regardless of living in the mountains, she had never truly belonged there. She had always played it safe. Not Billy. Billy moved effortlessly from the chaos of cities, superhighways, and airports to solitary days guiding a Jeep across an endless empty expanse of desert, or bumping along nonexistent roads in the African outback through territories where the game changed so often danger was part of the appeal. Nothing ever fazed him.

A knock on the door announced her meal, and a young man backed into the room with a cart. He placed the tray on the dark wood table beside the window.

"Khorb khun krap," he said and bowed.

She nodded, embarrassed that she had not bothered to pick up even the most rudimentary of Thai phrases before setting out. She had indulged in Vanity Fair and bad movies for the first leg of the flight and dosed herself on muscle relaxants for the second. Everything still had a rabbit hole feel to it. Violet slid deep into the armchair and ate every bite of the silver bean thread salad. Downing nearly a liter of water, she gazed out at the cityscape below. She hadn't expected skyscrapers. Over the last few months, each time she had tried to visualize the journey ahead she'd envisioned hardships in barren landscapes. Yet, here was Bangkok, beckoning. Still, she wasn't quite ready for the Patpong night market or a sex show—not that she wasn't curious about the whole Ping-Pong ball thing—but it was Christmas, for fuck's sake. She climbed back into bed, and that night she slept the sleep of the dead.

In the morning, the concierge assured her there were several Internet points nearby. She left the splendor of the hotel and walked in the crippling heat through the chaos of Bangkok, moving slowly along the crowded sidewalk, alarming tangles of electrical cable spiraling like concertina wire on the facades of buildings. The air was palpable, thick with exhaust and dense with the pervasive scent of steaming noodles, sticky with tamarind and tossed in massive street-side woks. She found the city repulsive and utterly compelling, the sheer volume of people and the pace overwhelmed her, and the sound of the Thai language made her feel off-kilter.

She wandered through an area riddled with market stalls. Row after row of bootleg DVDs and knock-off designer handbags, luggage, and clothing of every type. Buddha-inspired knickknacks were everywhere—

Sitting Buddha, Standing Buddha, Reclining Buddha. So many Buddhas, so little time, she thought, eschewing the plump deity to look at the sarongs instead. It was too early in the journey to buy anything. If she started shopping now, her dreaded backpack would soon weigh more than she did. She continued back down the sidewalk past slender Thai boys hustling and still younger girls walking arm-in-arm with aging Western men, puffy and sunburned, their shirts invariably unbuttoned one notch too many.

She came upon the tableau of a raven-haired girl nursing an infant, her brown legs and bare feet curled beneath her on the sidewalk, a Styrofoam cup with nothing to weigh it down tipped over beside her knee. The girl was filthy and so achingly beautiful that Violet was unable to hold her gaze. Men and women rushed past carrying briefcases and shopping bags without so much as a glance, making their way up the stairs to the Blue Line overhead. Tuk-tuks, taxis, and motorcycles all leaned on their horns. The decibel level was unbearable. Amidst all of it: Kentucky Fried Chicken and Pizza Hut, Tower Records. Even Gucci and Prada, where snakeskin handbags and high-heeled sandals sparkled in the windows.

Violet bought a cappuccino at Starbucks and one of Billy's diatribes against The Man played out in her head. She ignored it. For all she knew this might be her Last Cappuccino and she pictured herself a Leonardo-like apostle at the espresso altar. On the next block, she slipped into the cool of an Internet café, cardboard cup clenched in hand. Inside, everyone was abuzz. A group of Thai customers formed a semicircle around a small television in the back. One woman cried and clutched the arm of the man beside her. She was nearly hysterical. Violet couldn't figure out what they were saying.

She sat down at the nearest monitor, typing in her password. She had been feeling rather smug about not having checked her email since Boulder. She hoped Billy would notice she had so calmly boarded her flight and arrived in Southeast Asia without a hitch. The air conditioning was a relief, but the fluorescent lights glared and the seat was sticky beneath her. She waited for the page to slowly load. The screen flickered reminding her of those first-generation PCs and prehistoric dial-up connections the rest of the world had forsaken but were seemingly de rigueur in Thailand.

Eventually, she discovered two emails from Billy, both with "Urgent" in the subject line. She read them in the order that she'd received them. The first simply said, "Don't leave without calling me. Something's come up." In the second, sent 20 minutes later, he wrote, "Violet, I met someone. I'm sorry, but I know you don't really want to make this trip, and she does—" Violet could not bring herself to read further. She did not know whether to puke or to cry.

She cried.

Another traveler tried to console her. He was lanky and English and wore a T-shirt sporting a shiny decal emblazoned with "Full Moon Party."

"I hope you weren't heading south," he said.

"South?"

"It looks like Indonesia may have taken a worse hit."

Finger poised over the delete key, she glanced at Billy's email. She was unable to fathom an appropriate reply and turned back to the man, puzzled.

"The tsunami," he said. "It's so awful."

"Tsunami?"

Back at the hotel, she lay in her queen-sized bed, shades drawn, the remote control in hand, watching BBC World through tears. All that suffering. And all of it so close by. And what the fuck was Boxing Day, anyway? She stared at the television with morbid curiosity, uncertain if she hoped to see Billy alive or dead. Should she report him missing to the embassy? Was he missing? Or would she flip open Newsweek in a few days to find images of the tidal wave with his photo credit below? Knowing Billy, no matter how much had been laid to waste, it would somehow help his career. He had a knack for being in the thick of things and coming out unscathed. But maybe his new girlfriend had been sucked out to sea. The thought filled Violet with a fleeting sensation of glee that quickly boomeranged back as unadulterated jealousy, seconds later reconfiguring itself as guilt. Get a-fucking-hold of yourself, she said. Her voice sounded strange in the empty room. All Violet could think about was the fact that Billy had dumped her.

Over and over the television screened the same terrifying clips of the tsunami. Relentless images of the eerie calm during the moments beforehand when the sea grew flat and the water receded, leaving the shoreline dry, the boats nearly aground, beachgoers wading in the shallow sea or curiously observing the water. Then, suddenly, a great swath of wave swirling on the horizon, moving closer, and closer, until the mad rush of water became an unstoppable current. Palm trees torn from their roots and tumbling as if they were branches. The tide gushing and rising and swallowing the shore, churning and dragging people along with it amidst tables, chairs, and even cars. Everybody running and screaming and scrambling to any high point they could find, beaches and villages instantly engulfed, their hotels and homes flooding and floating around them. Then the aftermath. Victims stranded and families separated from each other. One beachfront paradise after the next strewn with wreckage. Dead bodies bloating in the sun alongside strange species of marine life, unknown creatures now made manifest, hurled forth from the deep, tentacles twisted and decaying on the sand.

After she'd viewed the same newscast replayed countless times, she got up and searched through her things for her ticket. Her flight back to Colorado was from Venice. In six months. Her house was rented. Her leave of absence approved. Her temporary replacement hired and already sitting at her desk. Violet had nowhere to go. She called down to the lobby and asked if someone could deliver cigarettes and a lighter. She hadn't smoked in years, but she intended to start back up. Once the package arrived, she swaddled herself in the silky sheets, propped up against several plush pillows. Only a small crack of light found its way through the heavy curtains. The hotel was silent. She heard nothing. Not the other guests coming in and out or opening and closing doors along the hallway, nor the elevator's ding as it arrived on her floor, not a peep from the world beneath her window. She was hermetically sealed into her deluxe suite, clutching the packet of cigarettes until day became night, finally opening it and coaxing one out of the pack. The smell of tobacco was familiar, simultaneously delicious and awful, and she lit the forbidden cigarette, watching the ash burn down toward her fingers, then lighting another.

Violet felt hollowed out, incapable of producing any meaningful response or emotion. She smoked and watched the footage in English, then flipped to Star TV Asia and watched it in Thai, then German, still later in French. She looked at the television until she was certain she wouldn't be able to cope with one more second of it and then another hour would pass. She kept a kind of vigil, waiting for an impossible glimpse of Billy, surfing from channel to channel, then back to BBC World, until she finally shut off the sound. It didn't matter what they said. An earthquake somewhere in the middle of the Indian Ocean had caused the tsunami. It was a disaster of epic proportion. What else could they say?

She stayed in her suite the entire next day, only getting up when housekeeping knocked. She held the door open with her foot and grabbed fresh towels, a bottle of water. She considered an Ayurvedic massage in the spa downstairs, but she didn't want anyone to touch her. Even the slightest physical contact and she would surely fall apart. She found Billy's itinerary. The only thing she was certain of was that he had last been in Indonesia. But who knew where he might have gone from there? Or where he might have been when the wave made impact?

Using the hotel phone, she called Billy, again and again, but didn't even get a ring tone. She checked her voice mail at home in the States and on her cell phone. Nothing. She tried to convince herself that Billy was alive. She hoped he was. She even tried to pray that he was.

"Please, God," she whispered, "let him come back to me."

If nothing else, she wanted the pleasure of killing him herself.

That afternoon, she phoned her parents and let them know she was safe. Then she called Jane.

"I'm worried sick about him," Jane said.

"But let me tell you the rest."

Jane kept interrupting her. She almost sounded as if she'd been the one Billy had deceived.

"What's up with you?"

"Remember that time you were in LA and Billy came over for dinner? The night he got so drunk he passed out on my couch?"

"Yes. And?"

"I'm a little bit in love with him," Jane said. "But I'm sure you knew that."

"You slept together, didn't you?"

"No," she said.

"You slept together."

"Well, just the once."

"I knew it."

"I never wanted you to find out this way," Jane said. "But Violet, I have to tell you something else."

"Now what?" Violet reached for the cigarettes.

Jane began to cry, her words coming out in little choked sobs. "Kit ran away."

"When? Why aren't you looking for him?"

"He's at Kelly's."

"So, he didn't run away."

"Well, he ran to Kelly's."

"Fuck," Violet said. "Even my dog sleeps at another woman's house."

Her friend sniffled. "Technically, he's Billy's dog."

Violet resumed her position in bed in front of the television. As devastated as she felt, she could not cry. Her best friend had betrayed her. Her boyfriend had deceived her. Nothing was what it seemed. Of course she wanted to kill Billy. But that wasn't the same thing as wishing him dead. She didn't even wish his new girlfriend dead. At intervals, she sort of wished Jane dead, but the notion couldn't gain any purchase. The absurdity of it all. Even a self-proclaimed man-hating feminist like Jane was susceptible to Billy's macho charm. Classic.

But at this point, did it even matter? Just a few hours away, people were suffering from dehydration and shattered bones. Survivors wandered homeless and broken, looking for missing loved ones, their former lives irrevocable, their futures destroyed. Soon the entire area would be rife with dysentery and disease. Maybe Billy was dead. Maybe he had spent Christmas in a romantic seaside bungalow with his new lover and they had gone for a morning swim. She imagined a hundred scenarios, but in each of them the result was the same: Violet was left alone.

Soon enough, the images of the tidal wave were edited together in a snappy montage set to music, the news anchors speaking in serious but composed tones. The professional polish of their diction was infuriating. Tomorrow, she would go to the American Embassy and put Billy's name on a list of possible missing persons. Yes, she hated him right now, but she hated herself even more for not having already done so. What had she been thinking? Her stomach convulsed and she ran to the bathroom, her mouth full of that awful watery feeling just before vomiting, but she only dry-heaved.

That night, she slipped into a pair of jeans and a sleeveless top, put on her mascara, cried it off, washed her face, and began again. Finally ready, she fastened her earrings, took a deep breath, and closed the door behind her. The lobby was another galaxy. Her suite was lavish, but the lobby was so flawlessly appointed it felt like a theater set on steroids, some amped-up interior decorator's vision of Southeast Asian extravagance. Marble floors and ornate tables dwarfed by towering glass vases hosting enormous stalks of crimson ginger, birds-of-paradise and tall twists of bamboo, orchids of every size and color. Well-heeled guests sat in clusters on shapely sofas, women in strapless sundresses and men clad in pastels, sipping cocktails and leaning against magenta silk pillows decorated with Jim Thompson's famous elephant designs. All was luxury and five-star pampering. The staff never looked her in the eye, each one of them placing their palms and fingertips together before their faces and bowing whenever she approached with even the simplest of requests. There was a hush in the hotel; nobody spoke about the tsunami, nobody read, nor even held, a newspaper that recounted the rising number of dead.

Turns out December is actually the cruelest month, she thought. She'd once taken a semester of poetry and memorized "The Waste Land." During the early days with Billy, she'd even recited it for him. She knew it was a cheap party trick, believing he was like all those Boulder boys—easily impressed—and counting on the certainty that a good read meant nothing more to him than knocking back a cold one and thumbing through the pages of a Patagonia catalog. But Billy had never forgotten it, bragging about her to his buddies, even urging her to perform the poem for his pals. And, like an idiot, she'd always indulged him, spitting out stanzas on command. Violet cringed at the thought. Only now could she admit to herself that the feat was no more impressive than Kit racing to retrieve his ball or raising a paw when Billy barked "high five" at the hapless hound.

Realization or no, those lines of Eliot came flooding back to her as the hotel doorman helped her into the back of a cab. *At the violet hour, when the eyes and back / Turn upward from the desk, when the human engine waits / Like a taxi throbbing waiting.* Was she like the character in the poem? A blind Tiresias throbbing between two lives? Why hadn't she been able to see the life she'd constructed with Billy for what it was? Violet sighed. She pressed her hand against the cool glass of the window to steady herself, looking out past her own reflection at the density of traffic. It was getting late, but Bangkok didn't seem to shut down. She was acutely aware that she had no place to go. The taxi idled. The meter ticked. The minutes dragged. Violet bobbed between rancor and desolation. It took all she had not to burst into tears.

She composed herself and asked the driver if he could simply show her the sights. She listened to the unfamiliar sound of Thai music coming from the radio and stared out at the backdrop of strange golden spirals, the temples of the Royal Palace, and the enormous framed icons along the motorway. In the midst of several lanes of traffic were towering images of the Thai king in various poses. Dressed in ornate robes in one, wearing a polo shirt and holding a tennis racket in the next, then later beside his queen, their copper-colored royal mutt, Tongdaeng, seated at their feet. She recalled Billy's insistence that she leave the dog with Kelly; even then, he must have known something was up. Asshole.

She felt claustrophobic. Motion sickness, the bane of her existence, began to set in. She needed air. She needed to get out of the taxi and walk around. The only destination Violet could think of was the Khaosan Road. She had once rented *The Beach* and Billy had scoffed, telling her the Thai people were fond of wearing Leonardo DiCaprio T-shirts plastered with images of the actor, his smile revealing bloody fangs. They blamed DiCaprio and the production crew for destroying Ko Phi Phi, the island where much of the movie had been filmed. Of course, now it made no difference. Ko Phi Phi was toast. She thought about Billy's hipper-than-thou posturing, his been-there-done-that blasé whenever he recounted tales of working abroad, whether he'd been documenting the Rohingya people in Myanmar or photographing a yoga retreat in Bali. It made her ill. And she was nauseated to begin with. And yet. He was Billy. He was her Billy. Or, at least he used to be.

The length of the Khaosan was bathed in neon and pulsing and had more than a deep whiff of desperation about it. The short stretch of road was crowded with clubs and cafés, music blaring from each of the venues with competing riffs, but the same drum 'n' bass thud all along the length of the strip. Vendors hocked surf shorts and bikinis, chopsticks and incense, or pushed carts laden with small propane tanks and woks slick with oil, surrounded by stacks of blue plastic colanders full of cilantro and hot red peppers. Small metal bowls brimming with colorful curry paste. Rows of dried squid, pressed flat and hanging from wires, looking like sad relatives of cardboard air fresheners suspended from rearview mirrors.

As she walked, she came upon the omnipresent Holy Trinity repackaged and sold in tourist destinations the world over: Bob Marley, Jimi Hendrix, and Che Guevara. People never seemed to tire of purchasing and bearing their likenesses, she thought, and Bangkok was no exception. Passersby from every provenance were snapping up the T-shirts with an intensity that bordered on cultish devotion. But clearly the real crowd pleaser here was Buddha, dominating the scene in every size and shape imaginable.

Violet stepped inside what she thought was a clothing shop only to find still more Buddhas. Picking up a minuscule figurine, she admired the surprising weight of it in her hand. It was a scrawny rendition, roughly the height and size of a cigarette and this particular Buddha looked like he'd been fed a diet of tobacco and little else. Still, she was drawn to the statue. The figure stood with one arm at his side, the other arm bent at the elbow, palm facing out, his fingers stretching stiffly skyward. He reminded her of a miniature version of the Ken dolls she used to play with whose arms and wrists never flexed in a natural fashion.

The boy in the shop came over to her, pointing at the statue.

"You no fear," he said. But it sounded like a question.

"As a matter of fact, I do know fear," she told him.

She had to admit the truth. She was terrified. She had been terrified when she agreed to make this trip. She had been terrified when she packed, and terrified on the plane. And now, in the wake of the tsunami, she was terrified times ten.

"No," he said. "This Abhaya Mudra. Make fear run away."

She looked at the Buddha with renewed interest. Violet had conflicting feelings about her Catholic upbringing, and she'd spent the better part of her time in Colorado kidding Jane about being one of those faux Buddhists who flocked to Boulder, first attending the School of Massage, then on to the Naropa Institute to study who knows what. It irritated her when friends from Jane's meditation class would hover over their table at the Trident, dropping the words "Rinpoche" and "Shambala" into the conversation. It all felt so taped on.

Her aversion to his faithful subjects notwithstanding, she liked the feel of the slender Buddha in her hand. Under other circumstances she would have bought the figure for Jane, but her friend's infidelity had put more than a damper on Violet's gift-giving tendencies. Plus, Jane didn't seem to fear much of anything, not even the ramifications of sleeping with Billy. Violet continued to consider the Buddha, and the boy looked on, patiently, his smile beatific, his calm nearly infectious. Or could it actually have been the presence of the Buddha? This Buddha was too skinny to dispel much of anything, she reasoned, but she paid for him anyway, slipping the itsy-bitsy idol into the side pocket of her purse and stepping back outside.

From edge to edge the area was replete with backpackers and tourists, all reveling in spite of the tragedy. And partying alongside them were clutches of aging travelers with matted hair and faded shorts or sarongs, their faces like worn maps that had been creased and crumpled and folded too many times to count, excesses of pale skin scorched by years beneath a tropical sun and too many endless nights spent smoking and snorting crushed amphetamines off small sheets of tinfoil or dropping E from one full moon to the next—the inertia that had led them to the Golden Triangle cradling them in an ongoing state of disrepair, their visas overstayed, their return tickets never used, homes long since forsaken.

One bar was indistinguishable from the next, so she slid into the first empty plastic chair she found and ordered a beer in a bottle. Years ago, on a trip to Morocco, she'd learned the hard way about drinking cocktails with ice in far-flung regions. She took a sip, vowing not to speak of Billy to anyone she met. Across from her, three backpackers from Brisbane discussed the devastation, but they seemed more interested in scoring drugs and figuring out what island would be a good substitute. The one they'd planned on visiting near Phuket had been wiped out, the bungalows they'd booked through Hostel World swept away with it. The group soon paid their tab and moved on, and she sat watching the steady flow of gawkers and tourists, bar girls and street urchins and girlie boys handing out flyers for massages and guesthouses.

A tall, boyish-looking blond gestured toward the empty chair beside her and she nodded.

"Justin," he said.

"Violet."

Justin was from New Zealand, but his work for a disaster relief organization had taken him just about everywhere. He ordered a Singha and told her how concerned he was about the state of things. He seemed earnest, well educated, and thoughtful, but not so politically correct that he lacked a sense of humor. He was just passing through before catching his train south the next day. He would be overseeing the building of temporary housing, and he urged her to volunteer. They were setting up a center to administer medical supplies and help children reconnect with their families. If she were up for it, she could come along and he'd introduce her to his colleagues.

"You can always travel," he said. "But this is your chance to make a difference."

His eyes were a distracting shade of blue as he explained how easy it would be for her to sign on. He had a way of putting things that made her step outside herself for a minute, to see the bigger picture, but she remained noncommittal. Justin didn't know the half of it. Leaving the hotel had been a big enough decision already.

When she came back from the bathroom, the waitress arrived with two cans of Coke, a bucket of ice, and a small glass bottle without a label, setting the tray down before them. The Kiwi paid the tab and poured her a drink, reassuring her the ice in Thailand was absolutely fine. And as she told him the story of her life, or at least the last few days of it, everything began to go a bit soft around the edges.

"That's rough," he said.

She knew her breakup woes were ridiculous in the midst of so much tragedy. Nonetheless, she hoped she didn't seem overtly pathetic to Mr. Altruism of the broad shoulders and what was surely a washboard stomach beneath his loosely buttoned shirt. His accent grew more adorable with every sip of the Thai concoction. Listening to him, she thought maybe, just maybe, she could use a bit of disaster relief herself. Amidst the stereo reverb and the multilingual chatter, she caught herself fixating on Justin's large, capable hands as he poured more of the potent liquid into her glass. She picked it up, drinking it down in one go. For a moment it seemed to alleviate the confusion she was feeling.

She refocused her gaze on the large-screen television above the bar. In the crawl along the bottom of the screen, one dire statistic after another scrolled past. She searched in her bag for her cigarettes, and when she looked back up saw a group of refugees huddled together. Violet seized on the image of a man who stood with his back to the camera, a once-white T-shirt torn to shreds, his height and build almost identical to Billy's. The camera quickly panned toward the demolished coastline. *At the violet hour, the evening hour that strives / Homeward, and brings the sailor home from sea.* A moment later, the news anchor dominated the screen. Violet instantly doubted what she had seen. Billy was everywhere. And nowhere. An apparition.

Shaken, she returned her attention back to Justin, who was pouring her another drink.

"Everything all right?" he asked.

Her hand trembled when she lifted her glass.

"A bit of the collywobbles?"

She glanced up toward the television, but the bartender had changed the channel and a Black Eyed Peas video was playing.

"The what?" she finally managed.

Justin reached over and covered her hand with his, telling her what a fool her boyfriend had been to let her go.

She hadn't been with anyone other than Billy for the last two years, and before Billy, well, best not to go there but now, sitting across from Justin, the quintessential expat, she began to doubt that Billy had ever really been faithful to her. And not just the indiscretion with Jane. All those trips abroad. All those opportunities. She could see him now in dives like this one, disaster—natural or otherwise—looming over evenings fueled by high-octane booze, the proximity to death coursing through the body and being pumped back out in the form of pheromones.

"Have you ever traveled the Silk Road?" she asked him.

Justin nodded and she was relieved to let him run with the subject, which he did, recounting a long and circuitous anecdote about an encounter with a camel in Kazakhstan. She had little interest in camels, Kazakhstan, or any other place for that matter, but she was beginning to see the Silk Road in a different light.

"You're not thinking of going, are you?"

"I thought I might," she said. "Yeah."

Billy was alive, she was almost certain of it. But even if she were simply delusional, it didn't change the fact that he had convinced her to travel to the other side of the globe only to abandon her for another woman and leave her without a place to live. Violet was drunk. She was a woman scorned. But she needed a plan. And maybe just maybe she'd been right all along. The trip would do her good.

Fuck Billy, she thought. No, actually, fuck Justin.

His guesthouse was tucked between a slew of makeshift hostels, noodle shops, and massage parlors in a noisy, poorly lit alleyway on the second floor of a rickety building that surely violated every building code ever to have been implemented in Bangkok and all the ones that should have been. Justin pulled her to him, kissing her the minute the door shut behind them. They collapsed onto the small bed, fumbling around. As he began tugging her shirt up over her head, she realized she was about to be sick. She had never been a lightweight. Then again, she had never drunk Thai rice whiskey before. She rushed to the bathroom and he followed behind her to make sure she was all right. He was a tender sort of guy, holding her hair back off her face while she vomited.

In the morning, she could hear people having sex somewhere remarkably close by. It was difficult to open her eyes. She was so out of it she half wondered if it were she who was having sex and her whisky-soaked soul had flown up out of her body to hover like a mosquito net over the bed and observe. But no, the crescendo of moans now seemed to be coming from next door. Violet noted that she was still fully clothed, and she was instantly unsure if she was happy or disappointed about this fact. She peered through heavy lids at the squalid room. Mold clung to the walls in a Pollock-like splatter, and the floor was filthy.

She sat up slowly. She was sweaty and sticky and thirsty beyond belief. Everything felt tenuous and uncertain regardless of the violent sun that gouged through the window and fell in slashes around her. But one thing was clear: the Kiwi was long gone, likewise her diamond earrings, her passport, and all of her cash. At that moment, Violet was less sure than ever that she believed in God. And she still had her doubts about Buddha. But she reveled in the minor miracle that she had, at least, believed in putting her credit cards in the hotel safe.

If the Khaosan Road had looked bleak at night, the foulness factor increased exponentially in the morning glare of the Southeast Asian sun. Fortunately, she found a taxi without too much trouble. She couldn't decide if it had been good planning or bad that she had left her sunglasses back at the hotel. No, Justin would surely have stolen those, too. There was so much wrong with the predicament she now found herself in, it was best to just keep moving forward and leave the party autopsy, as she had once liked to call it, for another day.

The concierge would, no doubt, pay for her taxi—if only she could remember the name of the hotel. She searched around in her now empty handbag for the card and came upon the bony Buddha. So, the con-artist Kiwi had missed something after all, hadn't he?

She laughed out loud, clutching the tiny totem in her hand.

"You no fear," she said.

And like that, it was gone.

Cricket Boy

Cricket Boy has looked in the face of death. It only makes him horny. He calls me his Blow Job Queen and says, "Those Manchester girls haven't got a thing on you."

Four a.m. and the telephone wakes me.

I get up and go to the window, see Cricket Boy cradling his cell phone, the first snowflakes of inevitable winter fluttering around him. When I unlock the door, he stumbles down the narrow hallway of my apartment, knocking the artwork with his shoulders. I brush past him and climb back under the comforter.

He kneels beside my bed and says, "I only called you because I wanted to fuck."

"I only opened the door because I wanted to tell you to fuck off, but since you're here—"

Thing is, Cricket Boy can't get it up. I start thinking the reason for it is grief. His dad died of a heart attack three weeks ago, his sister died of cancer four days later. He was just off the plane from two funerals in England when I met him. But it isn't grief. It's Guinness.

He went straight from the airport to his neighborhood pub. I was there with my buddy, a writer who writes about women's feet.

Cricket Boy was slurring when he asked, "Got any English in you?"

I shook my head.

"Would you like some?"

I scrawled the writer's number on a coaster and slid it over the bar to him.

"Brilliant," he said.

A few days later Cricket Boy made the call, chatted with the foot fetishist and wangled my real number out of him.

"Your boyfriend said you'd be getting off work about now."

I knew it was him, what with the accent and all. "He's not my boyfriend."

"Perfect. So let's have a drink."

Not that he'd asked me on a proper date, but I hadn't expected him to be with four of his friends when I arrived. They were all artists, which is to say they were carpenters. I've always had a thing for construction workers—love, love, love power tools and the smell of sawdust, a beat-up Ford F250—good thing, as I spent the rest of the night being hit on by the carpenter-artists during which time Cricket Boy sat with his back to me and chatted up the waitress.

Dan bought my drinks and Riley lit my cigarettes. Boris tried to lure me into the bathroom with coke. Wesley managed to flirt with me while making excuses for his friend.

"He's had a rough time," he said, leaning a bit too close and brushing the hair back from my ear while he detailed the diptych of deaths with a whisper.

Around last call, I tapped on Cricket Boy's shoulder, "So, what's your deal?"

"I used to play cricket. Now I'm a contractor."

"Great," I said.

"Let's get out of here."

"Right."

Cricket Boy dances a little dance, waving a steak burrito in front of the dog. He's been MIA for over a week, then shows up after hours bearing a greasy white paper bag and talking about his trip to New York. From the looks of it he's only been to El Chino.

Cricket Boy has lots of ideas about New York. "The best cabbies in the world," he tells me, taking a massive bite out of the burrito and dribbling sour cream on the floor. "They all follow cricket—in Chicago nobody even knows what cricket is."

"Well," I ask, "what is it?"

He claims if he could see paintings at Boris's house like the ones in The Met that he wouldn't need to do drugs. Says he spent so many hours in the museum he had to buy his mate a lap dance to make up for it.

"Generous."

"Oh, you," he says, reaching to unbutton my jeans.

Later, in bed, he tells me if it wasn't for the rent, he'd live in Manhattan.

I tell him if it wasn't for life, he'd live.

The first time we fucked, we didn't.

I asked him if he wanted to talk.

"About what?"

"Exactly," I said.

I lay in bed beside him, thinking about death. Cricket Boy never mentioned his father, his sister. I wondered if this was how he and his hooligan friends got women in bed. One tells the sad sad story. The other takes her home. But recent death or not, Cricket Boy and I had yet to close the deal.

Waking in the turgid morning light anything seemed possible, and Cricket Boy got it going on. Then somewhere mid-screw, he lost it, and with the lost erection—the lost condom. Twenty minutes of groping and, finally, Cricket Boy signed on for the search, tugging the condom out of me, flaccid and pathetic, in his big working-class hands.

I've had a little bit of death myself, but I don't tell Cricket Boy.

Cricket Boy empties the seal onto Boris's ugly 80's chrome and glass coffee table and busies himself scraping out lines with a battered ATM card. Boris grabs the seal, licking the glossy square of paper for such a long time that I think the newsprint will come off on his tongue, but eventually he crumples it into a little ball and tosses it onto a stack of magazines, the top one of which is called *Juggs*. Gesturing at the assortment of porn, he explains that he only buys it because he paints the female form.

Cricket Boy, rolled twenty to his nose, laughs so hard he chokes, scattering the coke all over the rug. His face goes from its usual hungover British pallor to crimson as he hacks and coughs and waves his arms about, flinging himself back into a peeling faux-leather recliner and nearly pulling a Len Bias—or the cricket equivalent—in his seat. Still talking about the female form, Boris crawls around on his knees trying to salvage what he can of the disseminated drugs, yanking up bits of shagged carpeting and examining the fibers with his clever artist's eye.

When I'm reasonably sure I don't need to call 911, I take a look at the canvases tacked to Boris's wall and think, perhaps for the first time, that Cricket Boy may have had a point. Still, when I try to imagine him wandering through the galleries of The Met, it's a tough image to conjure considering the tableau he's creating now—sweating and jonesing and speed-dialing everyone he knows on his mobile.

Cricket Boy will take me nowhere, which I guess is where I want to go.

The second time around, same as it ever was.

I asked him if he wanted to talk.

"Are you taking the piss?"

"Taking the what?"

"Fuckin' Americans—can't even speak bloody English."

The writer and I are having coffee. He asks me what's up with Soccer Boy.

"Cricket, you mean."

"Yeah, him."

I stare out of the cafe window at a couple bundled in matching parkas. The guy is wearing a goofy purple fleece hat and holding a snowball, mock-threatening the woman with him. I shake a cigarette out of the pack and light it. When I look again, the woman's got the hat on and they are kissing.

"Let's just say nothing's up," I tell him.

"You mean?"

"I mean there is nothing worse than having a limp dick in your mouth."

"That so?" he asks, scribbling into his notebook.

The truth is I don't know why I've logged so many hours with Cricket Boy. Maybe it's the accent. Maybe I'm waiting to hear about all that death. Death with an accent.

Cricket Boy never wants to talk unless I'm asleep. He calls me late at night while he's eating take-out Chinese and watching television. I smoke a cigarette in the dark and look out the window, try to decipher the jumble words.

When the ad for 1-900-WET-TALK comes on, he tells me he has to go.

Outside there is snow, drifting over the parked cars and swirling in the blue glow of the street lamps. Right now it's beautiful. Tomorrow the commuters will unbury their dead cars with shovels and brooms, resuscitate them with jumper cables. They will pull out into the street, leaving behind them a wintry yard-sale of blue plastic milk crates and folding deck chairs, maybe even an ironing board, to save the parking spaces they've carved out for their return. Overly confident about the crunch of salt beneath their tires, they will flip through talk-radio channels as they hurry toward the expressway, a sheet of black ice beneath its snowy surface.

Mother's Day

She hadn't realized what Paris might do to her—the darkening summer sky over the Pont Neuf, the enormous rainclouds, backlit by the sun and reflected in the colorless Seine. The same colorless water crisscrossing the canals and quays near Saint Martin. And the uniformity. The even rows of slate grey buildings. The perfect coil of neighborhoods numbering the arrondissement. The symmetrical slope of rooftops, gunmetal gray and slick with rain. Then the shocks of color. Stacks of macaroons in patisserie windows, raspberry, mint, buttery caramel. Silver trays of sable biscuits dabbed with dark chocolate. A dozen candied apples glittering red and sticky on a sheet of white paper.

Or early that morning, discovering it was French Mother's Day, and buying peonies, even though she had no mother to bring them to—might never be a mother herself—longing for the Buckeye Belles, dark as menstrual blood and closed tight as fists, but something wouldn't let her buy them, and she settled for a few pale pink stems, the florist whistling and wrapping them in crisp brown craft paper, torn in even squares from a large cylinder and tied shut with raffia while impatient customers shifted their weight among overflowing metal buckets unwieldy with green-white hydrangeas and dozens of Virginia roses, creamy and full-blown, an echo of peach in the petals. Then later, the young Parisienne with a shock of magenta hair, scarlet fishnet tights, and teal blue boots pushing her toddler in a bright yellow stroller beneath the vaulted arcade of the Place des Voges.

Although they met in Rome, they had talked mostly of Paris. Over a decade ago they had spent three days together then parted, promising to meet in Verona and make their way north to Milan where they would take the night train to Paris. He traveled east for a gig at a popular haunt on the Adriatic. She headed north to the lakes and was quickly disappointed she had needed to prove her independence rather than joining him for the trip to the coast. She found Riva del Garda a little too much like Wisconsin and a lot too much like Germany— tourist menus with schnitzel on pizza. She sulked and scribbled in her sketchbook on the crowded shores of the pristine lake, all the while missing him in what she knew was a disproportionate way. She imagined him at the seaside surrounded by tanned Italian girls in bikinis. She willed the days to pass.

The ride from the Lake District in a tightly packed Fiat Cinquecento was bumpy and took twice as long as she had imagined. She sat wedged in the back between overstuffed cardboard boxes, a trombone, and a soccer ball, her own bag on her lap. The items slid and tumbled no matter how she tried holding the precarious arrangement in place. But she had been proud of herself for hitchhiking, something she would never have done back home. The Italians who'd offered her a lift sang along to the radio before growing bored of butchering the lyrics of the American songs that reverberated through the one tinny speaker propped behind her ear. She decided that the two men must have been a couple; they took such little interest in her, although they did seem intrigued by the man she was about to meet, at least until the conversation became too difficult for each of their limited vocabularies in the other's mother tongue.

The men spent the rest of the journey smoking and talking, or maybe arguing, she was never quite sure given the decibel of their voices, the ceaseless waving of hands. She had smoked along with them, impressed by the driver Francesco's ability to roll his own while shifting and gesturing, and upon discovering that the ashtray was overflowing she resorted to following their lead, holding the remaining embers out of the miniature window where the force of the wind sucked them from between her fingers and transported them into some roadside oblivion along the Autostrada. The singing, the half conversation, the rolling and lighting and disposing of cigarettes, it had kept her busy, busy enough so that it wasn't until she stood in the appointed spot in front of the Porta Nuova station that she allowed herself to consider the possibility that her new lover might not show.

She waited and waited, checking her watch, pacing and gazing at the people spilling out from the different trains and making their way along the tracks. She read and reread all the arrival times as they ticked across the board, trying to imagine where he'd be coming from— Ravenna? Rimini? Bologna?—then sat on her bag in the shade near the entrance, hopelessly inspecting the travelers toting their luggage in and out of the station. She had no idea how long she should wait. It had already been hours. She dug through her things for the phone number he'd given her, a "friend's place" where she could leave messages. She struggled with the pay phone and the phone card she purchased, eventually getting a dial tone and punching in the series of numbers. A woman's voice answered, "Pronto?" and she'd hung up too quickly, wishing she had at least asked for him, knowing she wouldn't call again. She convinced herself of the lie she'd arrived a day early, vowing to come back the next afternoon at the appointed time.

At the bar inside the station she met a Dutch backpacker called Jan. He was younger than her, but not that young—mid-twenties, she guessed, and well over six feet tall with shaggy hair. Stirring two packets of sugar into his espresso, he spoke impeccable English and lamented a missed train, having already checked out of his pensione.

"It's opening night of the opera," he explained.

It occurred to her that she, too, would need a place to sleep. They picked up a list from the tourist information counter and decided they better begin the search, walking in the late afternoon heat past sparkling fountains and shuttered shops, all closed for the siesta. They checked several hotels, even agreeing to split a room, no matter the cost. One-star, five-star, it made no difference. All were completely booked. They gave up and settled in the garden of a too-quaint café and drank beer from sweating pint glasses under the shade of an umbrella. When they stood up to leave, she realized she was more than a little drunk.

Outside, Verona had reopened for business, the streets crowded with scooters and cars and even horse-drawn carriages. An air of expectation hung over the locals, dressed in tuxedos and gowns, sipping prosecco at outdoor tables or strolling through the piazzas toward the Arena to hear Verdi. They carried picnic baskets and candles and by all accounts meant to make a night of it, eating and drinking and singing along. For a moment, she longed to hear the opera herself, to let the voices wash over her while sitting in that ancient amphitheater beneath an Italian moon. But she figured that tickets were as unlikely as hotel rooms.

"And it would be *Don Giovanni*," she said.

The irony had escaped Jan and they continued their ill-fated search, the night beginning to close in on them as they happened past Juliet's House, the last of the tourists clutching love notes and trying to press their way inside for a glimpse of the famous balcony.

Shakespeare probably never even visited Italy, she told him.

But he thought it was sweet that so many romantics made the pilgrimage. He admitted having visited her tomb the day before.

The whole thing's a farce, she thought. O, that I were a glove upon that hand—or however the line went.

Cars motored past them for what seemed an eternity, until a battered white compact pulled over; it was the second time that day she had hitchhiked. They were a young Ethiopian couple with two smiling kids whom she and Jan held on their laps. The woman wore a white scarf tied over her hair and had elegant hands, long lean fingers spread out over her lap. Her husband had on a crisply starched white shirt and a tie. The children giggled and played peek-a-boo with Jan while he chatted in Italian to their parents. She sat in silence as they made their way up a curving tree-lined road in the darkness, the summer air rushing in through the windows, the sky an unfamiliar shade of Mediterranean blue.

The gates of the former monastery swung shut behind them for the curfew and would remain locked until morning. Aside from the bottle of wine and the opener she had stashed in her bag, she was as ill-equipped for a hostel as she had been for the rest of this sojourn. No private rooms were available so she exchanged her passport for space on the floor in the women's dorm along with a towel, a sheet, and a pillow.

Outside, a group of Australians laughed and played cards, covertly passing a bottle under the table in the dark. She and Jan smoked a joint with two of the Aussies beneath an immense oak, the net of branches black and spidery above them. By that time, she was so high and drunk and humiliated that she couldn't decide which one of these men she should sleep with to get over it, but she knew she could have her pick. She ended up in the shower stall with the young one from Melbourne. To earn his travel money he had worked construction for months, and had tanned, muscular arms to prove it, but he also had freckles and auburn curls and was as opposite from her lover as any of them could have been.

Afterward, she wrapped herself in her rent-a-sheet, hoping it was clean, or at least lice free, and slipped into the darkened dorm, tiptoeing amidst the slumbering bodies until she found a spot near the window. She lay on the hard floor listening to the sounds of soft snores and breathing, wind rattling the shutters against the centuries-old stones of the monastery. In the morning she paid her bill, if you could call it that, and collected her passport. She didn't wait to say goodbye to Jan or the nameless Aussie, but walked out the long gravel driveway in the shade of tall oaks and pines to the road.

She has only been in Paris a few days, all of them rainy. In the Marais, the line outside the take-out window of Chez Marianne wraps around the corner. The stoops are too wet to sit upon, so a throng of people hovers nearby eating pita stuffed with falafel dripping with tahini and aubergine. She waits for several minutes behind a kissing couple before realizing she first needs to go inside and pay, which she does, losing her place in line. But she has nowhere to be and the rain has stopped. At least for the moment. She makes her way to the back of the line, receipt in hand, and tries to eavesdrop on the others, too timid to speak her rusty college French, but pleased by the sound of the words around her.

As she edges closer to the window, she sees a man strolling toward her. He has a shaved head and wears sunglasses, even though it is cloudy. He looks vaguely Caribbean and, on his shoulders, he carries a little boy, about four or five years old. Beside him is a woman who has that look about her all the younger French women seem to have, underfed with a careless sweep of long fringe in the eyes, an I just pulled this vintage leather jacket out of the back of my closet sort of chic. The child's shoe falls off just as the family brushes past her in the line of customers on the narrow sidewalk. She reaches down and scoops up the shoe, offering it to the man, who takes it out of her hand and looks at her an instant too long, then simply says, "Merci," and hands the shoe to the woman beside him who slips it back on the child's foot with a pout before they walk off.

Another customer taps her shoulder, reminding her that it is her turn at the window. She gives her ticket to the cook frying the falafel, but she already knows she will not be able to eat. She can see her own reflection in the glass. Her wet hair pulled back from her face only makes her look old. It begins to drizzle and she walks, the pita losing heat, as she quickly covers several blocks and tosses the sandwich into a trashcan near the Centre Pompidou.

It couldn't be him, she thinks. It can't be him.

The drizzle turns to rain. So much rain for June. For summer. She had not intended to go inside the museum, but she suddenly feels like an insignificant speck in this enormous city full of rain and romantic couples and French speaking families and she can no longer remember why it was that she so longed to see Paris.

As she makes her way upstairs to the galleries, the rain comes down hard, coating the curving atrium windows, the drops beading on the outside of the glass and obscuring the orderly expanse of the city below, distorting it into an impressionist study in the absence of color, Montmartre and the spires of its famous church a wet gray smudge in the distance.

It had rained the day they met in Rome, too. Tables and chairs stacked forlornly under dripping awnings. The desultory snake of the Tiber gone muddy. It had stormed for hours the night before, but the air remained heavy with heat and the next rainfall was just a matter of time. Of course, he had found her in a cafe. And although it wasn't an Italian aperitivo, he insisted she try her first Pastis. It was strong and she liked the coolness of the licorice flavor in her mouth and the pale amber color of the liqueur and the way the glasses clouded up when he added water from the slender carafe. Everything felt exaggerated—the summer heat and the strength of the drinks and even the relentless rain—as if they were characters in a modernist novel, except they were in Italy, not France. By the third glass, she proclaimed it her new favorite drink and it wasn't much more than an hour before they were kissing and fumbling with one another's clothing at the table, then rushing through the rainstorm to the towering wooden doors of a palazzo he happened to have keys to, practically sprinting up the wide stone steps and falling onto the bed and into each other, rain pounding against the windows, jarring the windows open, and sliding over the marble windowsill into pools on the floor near the bed.

They spent the entire afternoon and early evening unable to stop. Rome viewed through raindrops, through the tall arched window beside the bed. Even the grey sky couldn't dull the terracotta tiles of the rooftops or the fuchsia bougainvillea, wet and clinging to ochre walls, the green stretch of umbrella pines on the hill in the distance or the way the rainwater beaded off his long dark dreadlocks, onto creamy linen sheets and his dark hands closed around her pale waist, pulling her on top of him and holding her there, as close as they could be, till neither of them had anything left and they lay clasped together listening to the Roman rain.

It wasn't that long ago, or was it, she wonders. Everything seemed so much simpler then and yet it had all required so many complicated steps. There had been no discount airlines or ATM's, no cell phones or email. Slips of paper scrawled with phone numbers and folded into wallets or notebooks, so easily lost. Meetings arranged by date and time with no real way to confirm or cancel and no back-up plan. She hadn't waited for him on that second day in Verona, but hopped on the next train to Milan and then later on the overnight to Paris in a couchette shared with two elderly women from Wales and an Italian professor preparing a lecture for the Sorbonne. As the train rushed through the darkness, she resolved that she would somehow bump into him in Paris—even with its millions of inhabitants—she'd walk down a street and see him or find him in another café or scan all the ads for the clubs to see where he might DJ. It could have been a mistake. He might have been legitimately delayed. Italian trains were notoriously unreliable. But as the hours passed, Paris began to loom rather than beckon, and so when the train pulled into Dijon the next morning she tugged her bag from the overhead rack and stepped down onto the platform.

She discovered she was pregnant not long after she returned to New York. She had felt certain the child was his and not the Australian's, but either way, she made arrangements, marking the date on her calendar and waiting. She looked at all her drawings from Italy. She wanted to throw them away, but couldn't. She got back to work, saying yes to the first job her agent mentioned, illustrating a children's book about a cat that climbs in a child's suitcase and has an adventure. As she sketched the preliminary drawings she could feel that even her fingers had swelled and her breasts had begun to ache. She vomited almost constantly.

She hadn't been worried when their condom had broken—not about getting pregnant, anyway. She had learned her lesson about STD's in college and long used condoms, and she had continued to use them even after the week of her thirtieth birthday when her doctor told her she would probably never conceive, that her painful periods were caused by blockages in her tubes thanks to an earlier indiscretion. In some way, she liked knowing where things stood and she had considered herself lucky she wouldn't have to spend her thirties as her friends seemed to be doing, desperately racing to find a mate and get pregnant before the years clicked by, then watching their husbands dump them for a temp from the office or a personal trainer from the gym while their kids were still in diapers. She had never wanted children anyway. Not really.

But the waiting room of the abortion clinic did not inspire confidence. It was dimly lit and the air was dense with an antiseptic smell that reminded her of a veterinarian's office. She paged through a well-worn magazine. She knew what she was feeling was more than morning sickness. She looked at the clock. And she looked at her watch. She scanned the room. Nobody spoke. The carpet was frayed, the furniture dated. There was not a single window. She wondered why she hadn't gone to her own doctor about this. Why she was there with the teen pregnancies and the women on welfare. She got up and filled a waxy paper cone full of water from the cooler, drinking it in one gulp then crushing the cup in her hand and dropping it in the basket on the floor.

That first night in Rome they had forced themselves to get dressed and go out for something to eat. At the trattoria, he ordered without looking at the menu and the dishes began to appear. Fried Roman artichokes pressed like flowers on white plates. Spaghetti alle vongole drenched in olive oil and white wine and sprinkled with fresh parsley.

It was almost as if the more they ate, the hungrier they became, and it was well past midnight when they finished the last of it and an elderly waiter in a long white apron brought the bill and he paid it and they stepped back outside.

He knew the city well, easily navigating the neighborhoods and narrow streets. He had friends there, he'd said, and the apartment was his whenever he wanted it. But he told her he really only came to Rome when there was work at one of the better clubs, that he'd spent the last six months traveling around the country from one gig to the next. He didn't want to settle in Italy, though, and he'd decided on Paris, which was easier because he could get a French passport through his mother's side of the family. He found Italians too racist and he had grown tired of being stopped and searched in train stations and airports. Not that it had ever really been any different in the States.

"I'll never go back there," he told her.

The plane trees beside the Tiber glistened, but the rain had finally stopped and the heat had broken. He put his arm around her and she shivered more from his touch than anything else. They walked over a footbridge and stood on the Isola Tiberina looking out at the river, the streetlamps reflected on the dark surface, the water rushing fast and high against the embankments, small branches tumbling and disappearing with the current.

The Calder exhibit is overly crowded and it is nearly impossible to see anything. She is unable to get close enough to examine any of the artist's drawings. And she moves quickly past the sculptures, glancing at the way the shadows twist on the white walls of the museum, but not pausing long enough to understand the intricacy of the wire objects. She hears the excited voices of children as she gravitates toward a film of the artist's circus projected in a small room, but decides to skip it and visit Kandinsky instead.

She had expected the bold colors, the dizzying circles and geometric shapes, but not the horses. In Kandinsky's early paintings, blue horses gallop through brushstrokes of color. And it's the horses that do it. She realizes what she is feeling is happiness. To be in this museum. To finally be in Paris. Even if it had taken so many years to get here. She had always loved horses and, like many young girls, begged her parents to let her ride, but she had never managed to convince them, so she spent her childhood filling notebooks with drawings and reading *Misty of Chincoteague* and *The Black Stallion*. It had been a long time though—nearly thirty years—since she had thought about riding, much less drawn or painted a horse herself. She makes her way around the groups of people wearing audio guides clustered in front of the more famous works and goes on to see the rest of the show. As she looks at the images, surrounded by the quiet murmur of the museum, she feels something tight and knotted inside her begin to soften.

She had felt less and less anxious during those next few months. She had rushed out of the clinic telling the receptionist she needed air, but by the time she reached the end of the block she knew she wouldn't return. After all, it must have been meant to be. And this was her chance. She was not entirely confident about becoming a mother, much less a single one, but her career was going fairly well, and at least for the first few years, while the baby was small, she could continue to live and work in her studio on the Lower East Side. She was convinced the child was a boy and after the nausea passed she grew comfortable in her new body. Some days she was nearly ecstatic. She didn't even miss cigarettes. Her friends all told her she looked radiant and for the first time in her life she believed she might be. The more her belly swelled the more everything began to make sense.

Coming out of the women's bathroom on the main floor of the Pompidou, she sees the young woman whose child had lost his shoe. Mother and son wait in line behind a dozen or so others. She quickly passes them. She tells herself to be calm. She tells herself to leave. She looks around the museum at all the people—waiting for tickets in the cue, coming down the escalator from the galleries, passing through security at the entrance, checking umbrellas and coats, drinking at tables in the café on the mezzanine. She doesn't see the man anywhere. Again, she tells herself to go. To walk outside. She looks toward the doors. Rain falls onto the pavement in gray sheets.

She hurries across the lobby and into the museum shop instinctively passing the postcards and cash registers heading toward the music section in the back. The floor is slippery from all the dripping umbrellas, the store crowded and chaotic and too warm inside. Someone has left an Yves Klein catalog open on a nearby table. She picks it up, glancing briefly at Klein's work in his trademark blue. She hears somebody speaking English and she glances around the store, but sees only a group of American college students standing near a rack full of guides and maps. She carries the Klein book with her.

On the first truly cold Manhattan night, after walking home from meeting the author she'd been collaborating with, she realized the baby had stopped kicking. That he hadn't kicked and he hadn't shifted position for what seemed like a long time. She tried to remember when it was that she had last felt even a nudge and she couldn't. But she knew it had been too long. She had put down her portfolio on the drafting table, called her doctor, and hurried back outside, hailing a taxi to take her to the emergency room. After the exam, they explained that even though it wasn't yet the end of her second trimester, her body would go into labor and she would deliver the fetus in a couple of weeks, but she elected to be induced as soon as possible. For the next few days, she thought of nothing but the dead child inside of her.

She sees him. Or she sees the man who had carried the small boy. She looks at him, his lean frame, his fingers gently flipping through the rows of CD's. She sees his smooth head and his unshaven profile and she moves closer, close enough to see the shadow of silver in his beard as she walks past. And she thinks she sees the older version of the man she met all those years ago in the Roman café. She remembers his long dreads, grazing his shoulders, and the way his brown eyes glittered with gold flecks, his beautiful hands as he took the lighter from hers and lit both their cigarettes, smiling and sliding into the seat across from her without asking permission.

He had called her once. From Paris. A few weeks after she had been induced and given birth to the stillborn, a boy, she came home to a message blinking on her answering machine. He apologized for not being there that day in Verona. Something had come up, he said, and it had taken him all these months to find her. At least he hoped he had finally found her.

"Call me," he said. "Please."

She wanted to believe him, and she wanted to return the call, but each time she lifted the receiver her body caved in on itself in sobs. That winter she had finished the illustrations and gone over the final proofs. The writer, like everyone else, was discreet and never asked her about the pregnancy. But sometimes she wished someone would say something so that she could. The story of the cat that climbed into a suitcase in New York and ended up in Rome was unexpectedly popular and the royalties earned her a lot of money. The following year she sold the animation rights. Everyone urged her to do the drawings for a sequel, especially her agent and the book's author, but she declined.

The man's cellphone rings. He reaches for it and answers without looking up from the CD cases. He speaks too softly for her to hear him and a few moments later he turns to leave, walking directly past her, glancing down at his phone, preoccupied. She practically drops the book she is holding and follows him.

She could call his name, she thinks. Only to see if he turns or looks.

But just outside the bookstore she stops and stands perfectly still in the massive lobby beneath the high industrial ceiling with its silver and blue latticework of ducts and interlocking tubes and she watches the man slip the phone into his back pocket and move gracefully through the crowd of people toward the young woman and the small boy who wait for him near the tall glass doors. The boy takes his father's hand and the three of them walk outside into the gray light, the Paris rain.

She descends the narrow steps of the metro, the hems of her trousers dark with wet and her shoes soaked through from an afternoon of inescapable puddles. She hopes the train will get her close. She unfolds her map and studies it, then forsakes it, opting to exit at the next stop. She emerges not far from Boulevard de Belleville where she walks slowly along past a Chinese grocer, a kosher butcher, and a Tunisian bakery, and on through the closed market stalls to an area where clusters of Algerian men haggle over old radio parts and indecipherable bits of machinery spread on plastic trash bags and damp newspapers beneath the tall trees.

The air is gray mist as she turns off, heading down the Rue Timbaud where she finds herself amidst a group of giggling young black kids wobbling at an improbable height on makeshift stilts, their feet balanced on narrow pegs, shoes bound in place with electrical tape. Their big brother and sister-aged counterparts prop them up, spotting them from below, the stilt-walkers making tentative progress among owners with small dogs on leashes and customers exiting a bakery, the requisite baguette tucked under their arms. She continues on and begins to notice a shift in the storefronts to the funky clothing stores and crowded cafés that populate the streets of the 11th in and around Rue Oberkampf and she knows that she is close to the attic apartment she has rented.

The surprise of sunlight through dormer windows, after a day of rain, after walking for hours in rain, after climbing the spiral of sagging wooden stairs, shaking the raindrops from her umbrella and jiggling the lock to make her way inside. The air feels close and warm. She looks around the room at all the books and objects that don't belong to her. In a vase beside the bed are the peonies she had purchased earlier that morning; the blossoms have now fully opened and already begun to shed, petals scattered, a translucent pink against the dark wood floor. She picks up the petals cupping them softly in the palm of one hand and moves to the windowsill, blinking in the unexpected brightness, and throwing the window open to the clatter of dishes from neighbors leaning over kitchen window sinks, the strains of hip-hop pulsing several floors below and the sound of a baby crying somewhere across the courtyard.

Dog Boy

I fucked Dog Boy because I hated his girlfriend's shoes. It wasn't about lust—not that I didn't lust after him (everybody did)—and it wasn't about love, not to begin with, no, but what's not to love about a half Spokane, half Swedish bartender attended by a pack of female dogs (each named for a different woman in his life, yet none of them called bitch)? And how could I resist him leaning across the bar toward me, his long auburn hair draped down his back, damp with the resiny scent of his girlfriend's Aveda shampoo, that slight slant of the head echoing his German Shepherd Sheba's, the cleanshaven cleft of his jaw in a city rank with goatees, smooth song of his abs once sighted when he tugged off a fleece and trailed his T-shirt up along with it, that split second of skin, perfect play of his jeans over his long lean frame. Yeah. And like that. But no. It wasn't really any of that. All that made the place appealing. The bar. Appealing. Nobody frequents a place because the bartender is a dog, right? And everybody knows which bar, so there's no sense naming it now that it's appeared in all those movies mourning a musical moment long past. But back then the scene was a decade away from becoming a cliché and I was newish in town and it was good to get in out of the rain, settle on a stool, sometimes circling the job ads, more often perusing "I SAW U" (nobody ever saw me) while Dog Boy dosed me with double espresso (by then even the saddest dive could make a macchiato—and it was a sad dive, if a soon to be famous one). Our easy routine, a too-tall mug placed on a clean coaster before me, the dogs, if not sniffing my pockets for snacks, snuggled in the storefront window facing the street. I needed those mornings, that semblance of stability, a fixed point in an otherwise gray world. I told myself I needed the dogs, not the boy. But there he was—there he always was—working the early shift, the place all but empty yet both turntables queued; each track he selected singing an arc over the bar—a Sub Pop sonnet slung from his bow, the blunt aimed at me—like an ex-voto offering to some shrine I was building but couldn't see.

So. The dogs. All four of them. Five if you count Jennifer's spastic Labrador Bailey—the-official-sorority-girl's-lame-pet-name-(not-to-mention-breed)-of choice. Oh. Bailey. Bailey, whose coat (chocolate, of course) and matching moniker might have foreshadowed the shoes. Jennifer's shoes. Dog Boy's girlfriend's shoes. And my inevitable reaction. Bailey, who reminded me of a three-day photo shoot for the not-so-low-octane liqueur bearing her name and how each day I ended up knocking back far more than my share of that opaque foulness thereby founding a new rule never since transgressed and perhaps the only one of my rules that can boast such: Never drink anything you can't see through. In truth, the rule should have been: Never drink on the job. But, here lies one (rule) whose name was writ in Bailey's. Anyway. The putrid associations with the sticky floor of the studio, the aftermath of so many takes, so much film wasted while I failed to coax the creamy cordial into a martini glass with its signature splash. A splash that could never succeed given the density of the drink, the shallowness of the vessel; the client huffing off set in tears, the art director swearing at the photographer, both refusing ever to hire me again. So yeah, Bailey's. Bailey. But not just Bailey—the shoes, too. And I haven't described them. I can't. Let's just say there were signs. Of course, there were signs. But I wouldn't be telling this story if I paid attention to signs.

Sylvie says I am the enemy of all women. I know I'm expected to embrace some sort of solidarity, that so-called sisterhood that would prevent one woman from seducing another woman's man. But get real. Debbie Deckert stole Jimmy Carlson away from me on a sixth grade Saturday afternoon while skating counter-clockwise at the Parkview rink. One minute Jimmy and I were hand-in-hand as he guided me on the turns, teaching me to skate backwards, then Debbie raced by in a pair of Bauer Blackhawks and carved a hockey stop in front of us, spraying an ice chip arc from the edge of her blades over my jeans. Jimmy dropped my hands as fast as he must have realized he was ready to drop me, and I fell to the ice finding myself eye-level with my real competition—the boy's hockey skates on Debbie's feet as she expertly glided away. Backwards, no less. It was an early lesson in putting your best foot forward and I had been doomed from the start in my sister's prissy white hand-me-downs. Cool girls did not wear figure skates. But Debbie wasn't just cool. She was a seventh grader, a bit of a badass, and she was fast—both on and off the ice. By the end of that evening, she was feeding Jimmy popcorn from her mouth into his, the two clinging in the glow of the fireplace, their legs and mutual hockey skates entwined.

I try to explain it to Sylvie—the trajectory that must have begun then and landed me here in the middle of this particular muddle, but even I know how stupid it all sounds to say a prepubescent skating-rink-induced footwear fetish could be a rationale for anything. She sits rubbing shea butter into the backs of her hands and squinting at the chalkboard even though she always orders the same thing.

"But really," I say, "the enemy of all women seems a bit harsh."

"Maybe not all." She is meticulous, coaxing the cream over each finger, massaging her nailbeds. "Okay, so the first time, shit happens. I get that. But still."

"You didn't see her shoes."

"I saw them. I've seen them. I'll concede they are unattractive."

Shasha, the waiter, waits patiently beside our table. We aren't really sure what his real name is and we can't really remember how we came around to Shasha, but we tell him we'll share the spring rolls and I ask for the green curry with brown rice and a beer and Sylvie says she'll take the Pad Thai.

"Extra tamarind, extra peanut, extra sprout?" Shasha says.

"And Thai iced coffee," she reminds him.

She never varies and he never forgets, but they recite their lines for the sake of continuity. Sylvie drinks everything iced, even in winter. She says the cold here is merely a suggestion rather than an assertion and I have to agree. Shasha puts the drinks on the table and Sylvie stirs the layered liquid so the sweetened condensed milk dissolves in the tall glass but now that it's concocted, the iced coffee looks a whole lot like Bailey's. The thought of it makes me ill. It makes me guilty.

Sylvie's just back from holiday in Playa del Someplace-or-Other where she tells me she ate nothing but ceviche, drank an excess of margaritas, eschewed advances by three men named Jesus but sort-of-slept-with-a-surfer called Kai, and all the while she wore white cotton gloves and anklets on the beach so as not to mar her perfect appendages. Nary a freckle to be found, but the rest of her is several shades darker. Inspecting her manicure, she runs the edge of her pale thumbs over each nail in search of a rough edge. Sylvie's a hand model. She's also a foot model, which pays better. Her hands and feet are insured by an agency in London, although she's managed to let the policy on her car lapse and she's always angling to borrow mine.

We met on a commercial when she swirled Dijon mustard on a hot dog. Or her hands did. Actually just her right hand swirled the mustard and it swirled the mustard on forty-seven hotdogs (that I had prepped) until everyone was satisfied and the client left the set and the gaffers stopped gaffing and the craft service people stopped restocking bowls of M&M's and I had packed up my paint brushes and knives and toothpicks and the rest of my kit into an oversized tackle box and the PAs started asking if they could take the leftover hotdogs home.

"So, you were drunk," she says.

"I was not drunk."

"You should really tell people you were drunk."

"What people?" I tell her, "You're the only person I'm telling. And you're not telling anyone, right?"

"The once and you call it a mistake. But you've been sneaking around for months."

"Nobody's sneaking," I say. "And there was only sneaking the first week and it was he who was sneaking not me. I don't sneak. I don't approve of the word sneak. Sneak is like the Latin root of sneakers. I would never wear sneakers. I don't do sneakers. That is the point."

"The point is you broke them up."

"Not exactly," I say.

Maybe I'm not telling it right. Maybe I left out a few details. Before the bar, before the double espresso, before all that, there were dogs. Or there was an imagined future involving imagined dogs. My performance on the Bailey's shoot hadn't done me any favors and business was slow. The Canadians were underbidding everything and jobs were moving up north, so I thought it'd be a good time to transition away from food styling back to my own photography, which had been the plan all along and which led me to the imagined—as opposed to imaginary—dogs. But I'd only gotten as far as purchasing an enormous box of Iams Lamb & Rice dog biscuits and telling myself there was cash to be made in dogwalking. Plus it would be good exercise. It would free up my time. It would be tax-free. Only I stalled out on designing the flyer. For days, I agonized over fonts until I decided just to place an ad. Then I agonized for a week over the wording of the ad and pretty soon I'd talked myself out of the dogwalking endeavor and decided it was decidedly beneath my skill set and that I hadn't paid back all those loans for grad school to hear the hurt in my mother's voice when she phoned to say she'd somehow found out I was walking dogs for a living.

I had only devised the dogwalking because I was trying to avoid the trap of bartending—the good money that is so good it is too good to walk away from, the late nights and the never getting around to your own work because when the bar closes there's always someplace nearby that stays open later and everybody's going there, and you know the late late night bartender, but that bartender is counting on extorting (albeit in a friendly way) all those tips you earned back at your own bar, knowing all too well that the fistful of dollars you walked with made you feel empowered enough to convince you to do your part to stimulate the economy and what goes around comes around and like that, so you order another and another and by the time the bartender pours you one last shot (this one on the house) you've stopped looking at your watch because now it's late late late and tomorrow's already a wash and you know you won't get any work done and soon your whole schedule is inside out because you're bartending nights at a bar in a city where, even if you do manage to wake up early, the sunlight doesn't seem to exist and the only thing you can count on is the cycle of interminable nights and endless days when the sky is so low it feels like you're living in some bad Blade Runner imitation of a world where it rains all the time and you're always using chopsticks and sooner or later you find yourself waiting for an origami sign of a dog or a bartender or a dogboybartender to save you from yourself, but knowing yourself well enough to know that you never pay attention to signs, you decided against bartending, and you decided to focus on your work, and you had already decided there would be no dogwalking, and you were proud of yourself for choosing a future without those imagined dogs, a future where you'd be saving so much money and drinking so much less and working so much more, but somehow it hasn't really played out that way and here you are spending your days in a bar, cause you've got to get your coffee somewhere, and it all feels sort of cozy and coy until the cute bartender starts picking up double shifts and he's always telling you to pass by, and it sounds like he actually wants you to pass by, and you know you really want to pass by, and so you find yourself passing by and spending all your evenings in a bar anyway; and maybe it's because Dog Boy is DJing, or maybe there's a show you can't miss, or maybe there's a rumor some band's playing a not-so-impromptu set you might want to photograph, and so now it's worked out that with all those days and nights at Dog Boy's bar you've ended up drinking more than you should and spending a lot less time in your studio than you'd hoped, and you're beginning to think that maybe you would have been better off bartending because at least you would have been earning something while you were staying out so late every night and maybe your dogwalking business wasn't such a bad idea either because just this morning you were walking Dog Boy's dogs in the rain, and not just his four dogs, but his ex-girlfriend's dog too, hence you were walking five dogs for free, and now you're totally broke because all the gigs really have moved up to Vancouver and you knew that would happen and even so you chose to forego all those tips from bartending and you also chose not to be a dogwalker, yet here you are a surrogate to so many dogs and, so yeah, like that, and beside all that, now your so-called work is suffering.

"It all started with those fucking dog biscuits," I say.

"Well," Sylvie says.

"And the worst part is Dog Boy doesn't want to have a dog with me."

"But you keep saying you don't want a dog."

"I don't." I tell her. "It's just—you know—a dog of one's own."

Sylvie rummages around in her Bionic Man lunchbox extracting a crumpled twenty and a pot of fruity lip gloss. "And so?"

"So I want him to wanna have a dog with me."

"You are some serious kind of fucked up."

"I never said I wasn't."

"And by the way," she says, "A trip to the pound isn't foreplay."

The bar is three deep when we arrive and Dog Boy looks the opposite of how I'm feeling, like all that sex we've been having has rejuvenated him, made him younger, more beautiful, more desirable, not just to me, but to everyone—man, woman, (dog)—they all want him more than before, and they already wanted him a whole lot, and somehow all that sex we've been having has only made me sleep-deprived and haggard, my clothing covered in fur. I have learned to curl my body around the shape of Mrs. Lopez (the Fox Terrier) and Trixie (a Husky mix), just as I've managed to deal with Philly (the Blue Heeler) sniffing my eyelashes and nipping at my socks. I've even come around to Sheba (the Shepherd) slobbering on my sheets. But bunking with Bailey while Jennifer's away on business is a bridge too far.

So, I'm trying to catch Dog Boy's eye and failing, yet managing to catch all the eyes on him while his eyes are not on mine. It is what it is. His loveliness was never up for dispute. He looks good. He looks better than good. And that can be dangerous. But I like dangerous. Problem is, so does everybody else. The place is so packed the fire code is surely being violated and I keep thinking the cops will come shut this shit down. And maybe they should. Shut. This. Shit. Down. I mean it's scary crowded. And the band—well, they rock—but they don't rock the way they did before the drummer OD'd. And I could use a low-key night is what I'm thinking. And DB is busy is what I'm telling myself. I weigh my crowd-induced-nervousness against a twinge-of-possessiveness penetrating a layer I could swear I'd soldered and sealed.

But too late, Sylvie is already leading me into the labyrinth, genius that she is at working a room—with her kid-gloved hands, her rosy crucifixion glow—in less than five minutes she's getting this one to buy her a drink (even though she doesn't want a drink) and that one to offer her a barstool (of course she wants the barstool). She may be a hand and foot model, but that doesn't mean she isn't pretty. She is. Maybe not as pretty as her feet, but most people haven't even seen her fabulous feet—this is not a slinky sandal city as you may have guessed. Anyway. The variety of pretty that Sylvie is sparkles, working its voodoo vixen charm on the crowd, which is mostly male and when it's not it's the usual desolation of dykes and guitar grrrl thrashers, wayward wannabes and Courtney copycats, but something about Sylvie parts the sweaty sea of them all.

With a smile to the barstool's previous owner that conveys thank you and confirms his act of chivalry does not come with conversation rights, Sylvie climbs up onto her perch. I wait for her dark magic to maneuver the guy one spot over out of his seat so we both have one. In the meantime, I slot in beside her, trying to ignore the hordes around us. Dog Boy appears bearing Sylvie's soda-with-a-splash-of-cranberry-extra-ice and the pale-ale-of-the-moment for me. He's got his hair in a braid that's more hunter jumper than French and looks superb but makes me suspicious. He pours two shots of tequila and lines them up next to our drinks and he's gone before I can lick the salt off my wrist.

"South of the border no more," Sylvie says.

She slides her shot my way, claiming she's in detox mode. I drink the first of the two tequilas, slam the glass back down just a little too hard.

"Not so much as hello."

Sylvie refuses to lob the birdie back. She gestures to the frenzied folk waving arms, hands, cash, anything to get Dog Boy's attention, all desperate for a drink.

But who braided his hair for him? I don't remember him ever wearing a braid. I stare at the second tequila, shoot it, then sulk into my beer, scanning the room.

"Stop picking the label," Sylvie says. "It's bad for your nails."

There's that hum that happens pre-show when everybody's overly amped and jockeying for a spot, some close to the bar, others near the stage. I've never seen it this full. Did I miss something about who all's playing? I look around, noticing that I see no dogs. They must be back at my place. DB would never have subjected them to such mayhem. In the corner near the turntables, I see Teak. He nods with a look on his face like he's trying to tell me something without telling me something. I can't see who he's talking to because whoever he's with is blocked by a dude in a sweatshirt with cut-off sleeves over the requisite long-underwear waffle, black hair long to his ass, and for a minute I think it's the bassist from that band I shot the album cover for—the band that never paid me—but it's not. Just an impostor. So yeah, it takes me a while to realize that a diminutive blonde bob is bobbing between the not-bassist and Teak.

Jennifer.

Fuck.

Sylvie's busy chatting with the resident of my future barstool about the contents of her lunchbox. I bolt for the bathroom before she unpacks it all on the bar. I've seen that number before. When I'm on deck, Teak finds me in line. The door swings open and he slips inside with me. All the chicks waiting roll their eyes.

"Don't worry ladies," he says. "The trigger's not cocked."

He slides the deadbolt and pushes me against the edge of the sink, gently, but with precision, like he's pinning a butterfly for his collection.

And I let him.

I'm irked about DB's non-greeting. I'm freaked about Jennifer but I'm more freaked that I'm freaked when technically I have nothing to be freaked about. And yet. I'm. Freaking. And I'm even freaking about the faux-French braid.

"How is it possible you ditched me for Pocahontas out there?"

"Dog Boy?"

"You call those mutts dogs?"

His eyes are like rain on moss and he knows it.

"I don't recall ditching you."

The thing is, I still like Teak. I just got tangled up in leashes. And now he's tangling me back up in him. He leans in, his boots straddling mine, his thighs pressed against me, trapping me in a kind of arm-lock-cage between his biceps, palms on the wall either side of the mirror.

"He's always had a thing for older women," Teak says.

"Ouch."

It's the only answer I can come up with that isn't an expletive. I'm not yet sure who I should be telling to fuck off, so I go easy on him. But Teak's not going the least bit easy on me. He kisses me hard on the mouth—I can smell him and he smells good, like cedar and smoke, as opposed to teak and smoke. (Cause who the hell knows what teak smells like?). Let's call it woody. Or would it be woodsy? Anyway. I tell myself not to kiss him back but I do kiss him back and he bites my lower lip between his teeth, tugging for a moment, which hurts and is also sending me somewhere it shouldn't. Somewhere that all of a sudden I'd very much like to go. Then he releases it, and pulls back far enough to look at me.

"Whereas I'm age appropriate," he says.

Wait. Wait a second. One kiss. And I forget everything.

"Jennifer?"

"Undergrad," he says.

And he tells me I'm in the shit. And he tells me Dog Boy will never leave Jennifer for good. Only he doesn't call him Dog Boy, he calls him "Everybody's Favorite Bartender." And he tells me, Jennifer's got one of those killer tech jobs and she's buying a mansion next door to you-know-who. And he says the company she works for is gonna explode. She's got Dog Boy by the proverbial collar is what he's saying.

And he says, "Do you want me to wait while you pee?"

There's no sense in telling what happens next. But what would you think—what could you think—if I tell you Teak and I conjugate the verb before we leave the WC? Or what if I say that we didn't but we might as well have because when we step out into the throng, there's Dog Boy, only his gaze is no longer averted, meaning he only has eyes for me, but seeing me come out of the bathroom with Teak, he turns away, and in that turning something slams shut inside him? What if I simply say things got messy?

I soon discover Sylvie has indeed commandeered the barstool we'd reconnoitered, but who do you think is stationed upon it? Jennifer. Right. Perfect. And the two sit talking (who knows how) while the band screeches into a set so loud it becomes legendary and not only because Dog Boy's bar-back Mirko records a bootleg version of the show, the sales of which later land him in a lawsuit. But who cares about all of that? Sylvie is talking to Jennifer! Our Lady of Lame Shoes. St. Jennifer of Software. Jennifer whose dubious taste has had no impact whatsoever on her ability to earn a shit-ton of money.

And I've been walking her dog—not just so to speak.

So what's a girl to do? Dive into the mosh pit? Drink herself into a stupor? Find the door, fuck off all the way home? Or fold her fingers into her palm before reaching out to pet the beast? My problem is I'm incapable of choosing the path of least resistance. Well, one of my problems. In truth, choosing any path is an issue. But I'm on one now, weaving my way through the crowd back to the bar.

I look over my shoulder and Teak is watching me. I look ahead and Dog Boy is watching me. Each wears an expression that reminds me of the time I drove into a blizzard on Rabbit Ears Pass. The Clash throbbing the speakers. Sudden apparition of flares and orange pylons in the whirling white, glimpse of a figure alongside the road, arms wheeling, and the way I'd never learned to pump the brakes rather than slam on them, but even if I had learned, my car was already sketching a sideways S on a sheet of black ice, sliding toward the cliff edge. Of course, if I'd tumbled over I wouldn't be thinking about it now, but it was a spectacular crash—into the lone tree that could have saved me. But there are no trees now. Not even a slender branch to grasp at for purchase.

"Sylvie tells me you're a food stylist."

I'd like to say Jennifer's tone is smug but the fact that I can hear her at all is a miracle. Maybe she's just being nice. Behave, I tell myself. My grade school report card remonstrance ("does not play well with other children") still dogging me.

"Photographer."

"Like portraits?" she says.

"Um—" I say.

"Or weddings?" Already the definition of perky, she seems to particularly perk up at the thought.

"Uh—"

"Commercial work." Sylvie throws me a bone, waving her dazzling digits. "I'm a hand model. We met on a shoot."

"Oh—Ohhhh." Jennifer says. Relief reconfigures her expression. "You're such a cute couple."

Sylvie takes a big sip of her soda.

I gaze down at my boots. Lesbian boots, apparently.

"I was worried one of you was the woman who's been chasing my boyfriend."

"Fucking your boyfriend is more accurate," I say.

Jennifer winces.

"Mon dieu." Sylvie says.

"She just left, actually."

"Yeah," Sylvie says. "Bitch."

"Totally," I add.

The singer belly flops into the crowd. Fans pass him round, nearly drop him, then tilt him back up on the stage, placing a bottle in one hand and the mike in the other. Teak appears out of the fray, flushed.

I say, "Baby, what took you so long?"

The crowd mentality is bipolar. Some shove their way to the front. Others elbow their way back out in retreat. Teak gets jostled even closer. He puts his arm around my shoulder resting it there kind of loose, kind of noncommittal. And even if he's only trying to accommodate his XL frame in the inexistent space it is, to date, the nicest thing he's ever done for me. I lean into him, start patting his pockets for smokes then remember he's quit. And so have I. Jennifer glances at Sylvie, confused.

When I look again, Dog Boy is holding a bottle of Stoli and several shot glasses, the bar stretched between us like Checkpoint Charlie. He sets the lot of it down, not deigning to look my way and he's gone, already working the tap. Pint glasses foaming over. Sylvie's glued to the scene like she's watching a horror film, the kind you wished you'd never started to begin with, but now that it's on, you can't force yourself to look away. I reach over her lunchbox, grab the bottle and pour.

"Nice braid," I say to nobody in particular and hand Jennifer a shot.

In the morning, the dogs all go crazy barking when Dog Boy rings the bell instead of using his key. I knew he'd show sooner or later. I was hoping sooner and stayed up much of the night trying not to dissect each scene that had played out at the bar. Not wanting to know if Sylvie had sprung her, "Do you want to play backgammon for sexual favors?" line on Teak. Trying not to imagine where DB might be spending the night. Finding no solace with the dogs, padding back and forth from bed to window to bed. All of us restless without him.

When I answer the door he's standing there, a puppy asleep in the crook of one arm. I think it's a Jack. Maybe a mutt. Petite and white with black paws, a patch over one eye. She's entirely adorable, but I resist the urge to fall into the cute trap. At least as far as the pup is concerned. Dog Boy's hair is long and loose but has those kinks in it that hair gets if you braid it while wet then sleep on it. And I wish that I'd slept beside him and been the one to tug out the tangle of his hair in the morning. I look at him leaning in the doorframe. The stoop is soaked from last night's storm, the sky a jumble of lavender clouds over his shoulder.

Dog Boy tells me he picked out the puppy a few weeks ago but it had been too soon. I think he means too soon after meeting me, then I realize he's just talking about what we talk about when we talk about weaning. And I understand that I am a parenthesis in a story that is already written. That he and Jennifer will soon be engaged. That Bailey and all the dogs will make up the wedding party. That Jennifer will invite Sylvie and Sylvie will attend, bringing Teak as her date and telling Jennifer we split up and red rover red rover she's crossed back over.

I run my palm along Dog Boy's collarbone and knot my fingers in his hair for just a second. Our faces are close together. Neither of us says anything.

Just then Teak shows up, taking the steps two at a time.

"Hey, man," Teak says.

He's holding two coffees in cardboard cups with plastic lids.

We all look at one another.

It starts to rain.

DB says he's just on his way out. I'm not sure if he's telling Teak or me. But the irony of the phrasing doesn't escape any of us. He kneels down and lets the puppy go, slides his messenger bag round and pulls out a bag of puppy food, setting it on the floor. All the bigger dogs surround the new entry, sniffing and whining. She rolls over on her back, paws in the air.

"Word," Teak says and, as if this had been his plan all along, "Could I get a lift?"

He holds out the coffee—my coffee—like some sort of peace pipe. Dog Boy takes the cup and they walk down the steps together, dogs trailing after.

The puppy squats and pees, then wobbles toward me.

A Roman Story

On the coldest day of the year, Pietro Pietrini wrapped his sixteen-month-old son Marcolino in a blanket, carried him outside into the brightest of Roman mornings and walked slowly along the snow-covered cobblestone lane. The young father continued up the steep steps of the ancient embankment across three rarely empty, rarely icy, lanes of boulevard and out onto the white stone bridge bathed in fresh white snow from the only true snowstorm the Eternal City had seen in over twenty-five years. Pietro leaned against the cold parapet holding Marcolino in his arms and looking down at him with a strange mixture of pride and fury. The child's face was red with cold, his wide brown eyes, identical to his father's, glistened with tears. But he did not cry out, nor make a sound. He had always been a quiet baby who rarely fussed.

One lone Roman walked his dog across the bridge and noticed the pair. He neither nodded in acknowledgement, nor glanced away, just urged his dog past. Salvatore Scaduto vaguely recognized the young man, but he was not in the mood to chat, much less discuss the weather. The weather was writ large over Rome: thirty centimeters of snow had mesmerized the city like a lullaby and sung it to sleep. And so he simply walked on, walking his muscular red Rhodesian Ridgeback on a long leather leash. The dog's large paws made the first prints of their kind in the deep snow of the sidewalk, a snow that yesterday morning had been a steady cold rain falling in wet wide sheets that quickly formed deep puddles and flooded the low streets on either side of the Tiber. The rain had continued throughout the day finally turning to sleet sometime during the siesta and with the darkening skies the sleet evolved into a heavy wet snow whirling slowly and heavily in the arcs of light from the streetlamps and over the frozen city, soundlessly glazing the monuments of Rome in iridescent crystals and tufts of white snow, unfamiliar, unprecedented, and some would even say unkind.

Man and dog walked on and for reasons Salvatore later understood—but at the time could not comprehend—his dog Zeno paused and growled uncharacteristically, then violently tugged on his leash, jerking the man back in such a way that he found himself facing the direction from which he had come. And there he saw Pietro Pietrini running across the bridge with empty arms. The man had not seen the baby fall—he had not seen that small bundle plummeting down like the heavy snowflakes of the night before, but he had heard—or thought he had—a creak like the cracking of glass and a muffled splash and when he looked below at the icy river he saw only the edge—or thought he had—of a pale blue blanket disappearing in the Tiber. He quickly clambered down the snowy steps to the river's edge, the dog keening at the leash and howling all the way to the stone embankment below, but Salvatore Scaduto saw nothing save fresh white snow and a thin layer of ice, broken and floating in shattered shapes on the surface of the dark water. The dog howled an otherworldly howl, burrowing his snout in the snow and leaning out over the river, pawing and crying and sniffing wildly. It took all the man's strength to keep Zeno from leaping into the water and when he finally forced the dog to heel, only then did he think to call for help. Only then did he realize Pietro Pietrini was long gone. And, of course, so was sixteen-month-old Marcolino.

The child had been swallowed by the Tiber, a river that had been named for a drowned Latin king and grudgingly accepted the job of watery casket to emperors and pilgrims, popes and criminals, and even criminal popes, for centuries, and although the river was no stranger to hosting the dead, it had been a stranger to snow and ice for as many years as Pietro Pietrini had been alive. Yet that same river would not, within a week, recall the storm or the ice or the way the snowflakes had been beautiful and silent and anesthetized the capital, bringing it to a slow frozen halt. For days afterward, Rome struggled as if waking from a dream, for the city was unprepared and found itself without plows or salt for its roads, and the Romans had all but retreated. But the snow and ice that had suddenly silenced the chaotic metropolis soon melted away and still the river refused to relinquish the body of the tiny toddler.

No matter how many hours the sirens scattered circles of light against the steep stone walls beside the Tiber and out over the surface of the frozen floe, no matter how many dives the scuba-clad rescue workers managed with their headlamps and rubbery suits submerging themselves in those filthy frozen waters, the search yielded nothing. For weeks they dredged and dragged the river from bridge to bridge to bridge. And for weeks, that soon elapsed into months, the neighbors, and even some who lived on the periphery, paid pilgrimage on the ponte leaving matchbox cars and teddy bears, lighting candles and writing poems, or dashing off handwritten notes. One young mother even referenced those legendary babes who'd been set adrift on the Tiber (and yet Marcolino had no basket to float in, no wolf to suckle him—no shore, nor den, would offer him sanctuary—and no city would come to bear his name), but those who came, came to believe in the presence of Marcolino.

They whispered his name and the stories spread. Some said his revenant swam with the surest of strokes. Some said a small figure toddled along the parapet of the bridge in the early morning hours gazing out at the barren black branches of the plane trees or dropping bits of bread to the ducks that had begun to circle the spot where he had sunk. Believers and nonbelievers, the curious and the bereaved, they all came and made offerings, wedging rosaries and flowers, pacifiers and plush toys into the white stone latticework of the bridge where the baby had last been held aloft by his father and glimpsed by a stranger walking a large red dog.

Pietro Pietrini did not like snow. He had skied just once—and loathed it—during a trip organized by his high school. He was one of only two boys in his grade who could not ski. His parents, Gianmarco and Giuseppina, had not taken him to Campo Felice in the Abruzzo on weekend ski trips when he was young. His family had never been to the mountains of the Abruzzo, nor any mountains, much less to Cortina or Courmayeur, to experience the idyll of a settimana bianca spent on the slopes. They were hard-working people who toiled to make life sweet for others in the form of pastries filled with berries or simple sugar cookies glazed with apricot jam. Their bakery was renowned for its custard-filled Bigné di San Giuseppe and frappe, those sweet ripples of dough dusted in confectioner's sugar and eaten during Carnival. Pietro Pietrini did not like Carnival. Even as a small boy he wished the Roman winter to end as quickly as possible. The cold only reminded him that he would attend no parties himself and that springtime was far off, summer still farther, and that he and his parents would be sleepless and exhausted till well after Easter. But every summer, for one glorious week in August, his family would spend their days on the beach near Torvaianica.

During the days before he found himself at the ski resort with his classmates, Pietro and his girlfriend Maria Grazia Bevilaqua had argued. She desperately wanted him to learn to ski. He had neither the money, nor the inclination, but she promised she would teach him herself and assured him he'd love it. He reminded her that his mother had not been feeling well and that his father would have to prepare and bake everything for Carnival on his own. She told him she had already spoken to his mother who had agreed he should join the group.

"Dai," she said. "Ti prego."

When Maria Grazia smiled at Pietro, he could not refuse her. They had been dating for years and the Bevilacquas had always been kind to him, but he sensed they only grudgingly accepted his role in her life. Still, they bought him Polo shirts on birthdays and expensive loafers at Christmas, and each summer invited him to their house perched high on a cliff in Monte Argentario, an invitation they must have known he could never accept, for as the years passed his family was forced to forego August holidays at the beach and keep their shop open to earn a bit extra. He longed to spend time with her in Tuscany after seeing her photos of turquoise waters and rocky coastlines, but was never able to.

Having convinced Giuseppina to allow him to make the trip, Maria Grazia set about convincing her own parents to pay his way and, of course, they agreed. She was a sweet guileless girl and the Bevilacquas reveled in indulging her. But the price of the holiday was too high— not for the Bevilacquas—but for Pietro. He had swallowed his pride and accepted because he wanted to please their daughter, promising he would repay every cent. He did not know it yet, but it would be the last act of generosity on the part of Maria Grazia's parents and he would never pay them back. And yet, it was not the loan, nor his lack of means, that would separate the pair.

Only Pietro and the Chinese kid whose real name was easily mispronounced and had long been replaced with the moniker of Rocco, were obliged to attend Ski School. Maria Grazia offered to stay behind and take the morning-long lesson with him, but he told her no, to go have fun. He was ashamed. Ashamed of his lack of know-how, his lack of cool, his rental equipment, and his wretched jeans, already damp in the knees from a fall he'd taken as soon as he'd stepped into his bindings. The skis felt clunky and awkward and his ankles ached in rented boots. On the bus the day before, Maria Grazia had given him a gift, a pair of ski gloves and their snug fit was a constant reminder of his debt unpaid. He shoved his hands through the loops at the tops of his poles, gripping them tightly so he would not lose control and watched her glide effortlessly toward a group of friends with bored expressions, all at ease on their skis, waiting in line. She climbed inside and the gondola wobbled up along the stretch of tall cables, taking her away from him.

Rocco Wong quickly mastered the basics, pointing the tips of his skis together to snow plow and come to an even stop, learning to plant his poles or to hold them as if he were balancing a tray. But Pietro simply could not get the hang of it. He had an athlete's lean, muscular body, but he had rarely participated in any sports because his family needed him to help out in the kitchen baking or washing dishes or sometimes making deliveries on his bicycle, then later on his rickety-old-fashioned Ciao! that had been his father's moped when people still drove the models you pedaled to get the motor running. His was the only one of its kind parked in front of their high school. Maria Grazia had thought it retro.

"Figo," she had said the first time he rode up on it.

Pietro Pietrini had not realized he hated snow until he visited the Abruzzo. He had never truly experienced snow, only the scattered flakes that fell and quickly melted every few years on a particularly brisk winter day. In the mountains, he was a stranger to the cold white roads that lead to the cabins where they slept, and he was uneasy in the lodge with its fake festive atmosphere, animal heads mounted on the walls. He hated all of it—the whole idea of frigid days spent slipping and sliding down a mountain, the feeling of icy air in his lungs. And he hated being an embarrassment to Maria Grazia. Most things had come easily. He had effortlessly attained good grades even though helping out his parents left him little time to study. He had always been a strong swimmer even though he only spent one week a year at the beach. But he had no talent for skiing. By noon of the first day he had all but given up. Having abandoned his skis, he sat on the deck waiting for the others in the glaring sun. Somehow he had forgotten his sunglasses and his eyes burned after a morning baptized by high-altitude sun, wet snow, and humiliation.

After lunch, he pilfered a Peroni from one of the lift operators and drank it while smoking a much-needed joint, hidden from the eyes of their chaperones, behind a copse of tall pines. He had only recently begun to smoke hash, a habit Maria Grazia frowned upon and one he promised her he would keep to a minimum. But he liked the absent feeling it gave him, the way it made the sun sparkle on the frosty bark of the trees, and the way it distanced him from the stress-induced panic that had grown to a crescendo inside him like a terrible clanging of church bells all morning long.

It only made matters worse that Rocco Wong had been given permission to hit the slopes while he was slated for an afternoon session with the 10-12 year olds. Although Maria Grazia wanted to ski together, he was obliged to stay behind so she set off for more advanced runs. That afternoon, it began to snow, and when she unwittingly veered off-piste, tumbling downhill for several meters, the new kid shushed over the bumps, gathered her skis, and offered her a hand up. Federico Montefiori had moved to Rome from Torino a few months before. Behind his back, Pietro and Maria Grazia had teased him mercilessly for his northern accent. Everybody had. At first. But Federico had an easy manner and he was quickly absorbed into the ins and outs of high school life. Just as he was so seamlessly absorbed into Maria Grazia Bevilacqua's life. Back in Rome, whenever Pietro had to work weekends, Federico was available to keep her company. Roman teens traveled in packs, so Pietro had not been overly concerned. He had loved her since primary school and for the last three years they had been inseparable. He had come to trust what she had told him: that they would always be together. But that was a child's wish and a teenager's mistake. By Easter of that same year, Maria Grazia and Federico were a couple and Pietro found himself alone.

That spring proved to be cruel in other ways. It was April when Giuseppina's illness became truly apparent. She had needed a biopsy in early winter and the results had declared the tumor benign, but within a month the doctors reassessed their diagnosis. Even radical surgery hadn't resolved things and she quickly resigned herself to the cancer. His mother, whose easy smile had always reassured him, and whose firm hands had helped teach him to bake, quite literally began to disappear. They buried her the first week of August, the week of his 18th birthday. Maria Grazia had come to the funeral, but trapped in the weeping arms of his Zia Giovanna, Pietro could only watch as she walked quickly and tearfully away, stopping beneath a tall umbrella pine and smiling a sad smile back at him over the gravestones.

Pietro decided not to return to school so he could work full time in the bakery, a plan he was never able to enact because his father lost their home, and the business beneath it, to a man named Sal who had foreclosed on the property. As they packed boxes, Gianmarco Pietrini finally admitted that unbeknownst to his wife or son he had been served eviction notices for years and managed to keep the truth from them all by borrowing money from the kind of man who did not appreciate it when you missed a payment. Without the daily rhythm of the bakery and without the singsong voice of his wife, Gianmarco grew bloated and bitter. He and his son moved to il Serpentone, an enormous over-crowded housing development on the outskirts of Rome. Noisy, neglected, and dangerous, their new home was an alien world to Pietro and the days loomed before him without work or school. He began to smoke more hash, telling himself that a joint or two a day was harmless. The number soon multiplied and he realized he might as well sell it himself, if only to cover his own costs.

By the following winter not even the lettering on the Pasticceria Pietrini window remained. Gone were the flaky frappe sold during carnival. Gone were Giuseppina's Bigné di San Giuseppe and the custard filling made from a recipe only she had memorized. Nothing that had ever been sweet in Pietro's life remained, not even the pastries he had oft resented baking and now acutely missed. Gone, too, was the sweet-brown-eyed boy who'd obeyed his mother and revered his girlfriend and who once thought that heaven was diving from his father's shoulders into the calm waters of the Tyrrhenian.

Pietro and Maria Grazia were both virgins and she had vowed to remain one. Pietro had never insisted, trusting that they would one day marry, but after she left him he quickly discovered others were more willing. He swore to any girl who pursued him that he did not miss her. She was spoiled, he insisted, a snob. But through all of it he knew that those years of attention from her had elevated him to a place he had never belonged and with her rejection, he had quickly slid back down the social ladder. He liked to think he was better off with these new girls from simple families, girls who did not plan on attending university in Bologna and graduate school in London, girls who opted to take jobs in clothing stores or nightclubs or who might, with luck, obtain their license to work in a dingy beauty salon that provided white uniforms for employees and bikini waxes to its clientele, those same girls who would discover themselves pregnant before they had turned twenty-one and would find themselves pushing a stroller across the broken pavement to the disheveled excuse for a playground in a nearby piazza.

Francesca had been such a girl. She spray-painted swastikas on dumpsters at night and sported several tattoos. She wore hair extensions and straightened her bangs pin-straight, cheering for Lazio, not Roma, when the football match came on. Francesca was not pretty the way Maria Grazia had been pretty. She was plump and painted and she squeezed her round ass into too-tight jeans and her wide feet into cheap high heels. Maria Grazia wore ballerina flats or Converse and had always smelled fresh like soap. Francesca's hair smelled of cigarettes and her skin was doused in too-sweet perfume, but it was not entirely unpleasant, Pietro thought. He had wasted time being chaste. And here was Francesca, sexy and pouty and always up for it. She quickly relieved him of his virginity and then some. She sent him nude photos with her cell phone and let Pietro Pietrini cram himself into any crevice or opening he could find, then begged him to come in her mouth. She let him do all these things, but she let the other boys do them as well, and eventually Pietro Pietrini moved on. After Francesca there had been others. Letizia. Fabiana. Chiara. Nicoletta. Too many to count.

From the outside, Pietro still had the appearance and quiet demeanor of the boy he used to be—his soft curls lent an innocence to his face—but his melancholy quickly gave way to recklessness. He began spending his nights stealing scooters and his afternoons disassembling them to sell the parts. Once he'd gained a reputation for having stolen scooters, it was easy enough for Mario, an older boy who lived down the hall, to convince him to help break into the apartments of elderly neighbors to steal cufflinks and watches and any spare cash they might have hidden beneath mattresses or tucked into shoeboxes high up on shelves. The following summer, during the dog days of August, it occurred to Pietro that his former classmates would all be on holiday and he could easily loot their homes for cash and jewelry, laptops and iPods.

Some days, though, when he would walk into a strange cafe in the early morning and smell a batch of fresh pastries cooling on a tray, he would feel a sharp pang. His mother had always told him when he felt disappointed or upset he should do something nice for someone worse off than himself, but the morning-fresh pastries were a terrible reminder of how long it had been since he had even considered such a thing. What was the last kind thing he had done, he wondered. He could no longer recall. He had been a good boyfriend to Maria Grazia, though, hadn't he? Sometimes he was no longer sure. He still longed for her. Once in a while he would drive by her parents' house in the Parioli neighborhood of Rome, but he never saw her. One autumn evening he dialed her number, still memorized though he had long ago canceled it from his cellphone.

"Pronto?" she said. There was never anything jaded in her voice and that was something he had always clung to. But he could not bring himself to speak.

"Who is it?" she asked.

As soon as he hung up, the phone began to vibrate with another call, the number blocked. It rattled him, but he answered.

"Aò, ma che fai?" It was Bruno Martinello, his only friend from the old neighborhood. Bruno convinced him to come out and meet him for a beer, promising him Testaccio would be swarming with hot American college students who wanted nothing more than to sleep with a man whose name ended in a vowel.

"Maddai," Pietro said, "you're kidding." But he agreed to join him and the two young Romans met a group of American girls with shiny hair, strappy sundresses, and flip-flops even though the evenings had turned cool. He had never understood the barrage of foreigners touring his city and he had never been drawn to them, but he suddenly liked the idea of conquering an American student. The taller one in the blue dress was named Mimi Jackson and she was the only one in the group who spoke any Italian. Bruno zeroed in on a brunette and lured her out onto the dance floor. Before Pietro knew it, each of the girls had paired off with somebody, leaving Mimi batting her eyelashes and waiting for him to buy her a cocktail. He had already spent more than he wanted to that night, so he offered to roll her a cigarette, which she accepted, leaning over for him to light it and allowing him a glimpse of her small breasts beneath the sheer blue fabric of her dress. Dio, he thought. What do I say to her?

"Sei di Roma?" she asked, saving him.

"Romano di Roma."

She explained she was from San Diego, an Italian Studies minor. Their banter fizzled out quickly and again he thought, Che cazzo ci faccio qua? Then he reminded himself, American girls love Italians. She just told you she loves anything Italian. And so he leaned over and brushed the hair back from her cheek and covered her mouth with his. She kissed him back, timidly at first, but by the time Bruno returned with her friend, Pietro was trying to figure out where he could have sex with Mimi. His old man would be home. He could never bring *this* girl *there*. Bruno had a car, but he was probably maneuvering the brunette into it himself.

In the end, Pietro offered Mimi a ride home on his Vespa. He had upgraded from the moped of his high school days. On the way, he made sure to take lots of curves so Mimi would be forced to hold him tight, which she did, laughing with glee the entire way. When they arrived in front of her building on Viale di Trastevere, he looked at her and realized how truly innocent she seemed. Suntanned and freckled and exactly what you might imagine an American studying in Rome to be. Long blonde waves of hair cascading down her back. Occhi azzurri. There was nothing about her that reminded him of the Italian girls he had known. Nothing. And as cynical as he had been all night, once he held her little blue dress in his hands and saw her standing before him in her white cotton panties and bra his world shifted ever so slightly. He felt lucky. And he no longer wanted to simply fuck her and leave. He wanted her to wrap her long American legs around him, pull her expensive sheets over him, and never let him go.

For the next three months his world was Mimi. He stayed away from home whenever possible and began making deliveries for the hardware store owned by a friend of his Aunt Giovanna's. He still supplemented his cash flow by selling small bundles of hash around the neighborhood, but smoked less of it himself. Though he was naturally fit, he joined a gym and started to pay more attention to how he was dressed. The cache of Polo shirts from the Bevilacquas began to come in handy. He wanted to do right by Mimi. He wanted to have money in his pocket so he could offer her dinner or gelato or buy her a rose. But she didn't seem to notice what they did. Mimi Jackson was happy to be in Rome. She was happy to sit on the filthy steps of the fountain in Piazza Trilussa and drink beer or cheap wine out of a plastic cup. She was happy to ride behind Pietro on his Vespa and see the city aglow by night. She was happy to let him sleep over and proud to have a cappuccino with him at the bar downstairs before she dashed off to class. Mimi was happy. And she made Pietro happy, too.

One morning, she had to get up early to study for exams. She shut off the alarm and whispered to him to make sure the door locked when he pulled it shut, leaving him in the darkened room. After she had gone, he could not sleep. He listened to her roommates rattling around and using the hairdryer. He waited until the apartment grew quiet and the door slammed for a third time before he shuffled out into the living room in his underwear. Two laptops sat on the coffee table, both open to Facebook. The apartment was in disarray. He wandered into the kitchen to get something to drink, but he could not find a clean glass and there was no dish-soap, so he gave up and drank directly from a bottle of water he found in the fridge. In the bathroom, the girls had left jewelry. Diamond stud earrings and a turquoise ring on the shelf by the mirror, a gold watch on the edge of the sink. Mimi, herself, had left a wad of rumpled euro on the bedside table. The laptops alone would bring enough money to float him for a while. But, no, what was he thinking? Mimi would know he had taken them. He guiltily slipped into his jeans, pulled his shirt over his head, and grabbed his jacket, bolting out of the apartment and feeling relieved when the lock clicked as he pulled the door shut behind him.

On the elevator he realized that most of the building was occupied by students. What if he were to take something from a different apartment? Mimi would never know. Nobody had to know. And anyway, all these Americans were so spoiled with all their gadgets and their Ryan Air tickets and weekend trips. They could easily buy new computers and cell phones, he told himself—they all used their parents' credit cards. He stepped out of the elevator on the floor below as three boys got on, then another came racing out from an apartment down the hall, calling out something unintelligible, before sliding sideways between the closing metal doors. Pietro Pietrini's heart beat quickly. He had not needed to exit on this floor. But he knew what he was doing. He walked with a forced nonchalance toward the door he had just seen the boy slam closed. He rang the bell. Nothing. He rang it again. Nothing. He reached for the doorknob and the door pushed open easily.

"Permesso?" he said. "Anyone home?"

The shutters were half-closed and the room was dim, but the apartment was a carbon copy of Mimi's. Again, two laptops greeted him, this time one open on the sofa, the other on the floor plugged into the wall with an adaptor. A black backpack hung off the arm of a chair. He unzipped it and began to slide in the laptops and the single charger, finding a digital camera and a passport with 200 euros tucked inside it in the process. He was folding the cash into his pocket when the toilet flushed and he heard the shower begin to run. Pietro left the passport on the table amidst over-turned beer bottles and over-flowing ashtrays and sprang into action, shouldering the pack with the laptops and quietly closing the door behind him. He took the stairs down to the lobby two at a time. As he got on his Vespa he heard his cellphone ding. A message. Mimi. He tapped, "Baci" into the phone, then buckled his helmet, waited for the tram to pass, and joined the morning traffic a little bit sick, a little bit smug.

Mimi never found out about the laptops. But she mentioned there had been "a bunch of robberies." Pietro had told Bruno what he'd done and the following Friday night when nearly all of the Study Abroads were sure to be out drinking or spending the weekend in Barcelona or Prague—what was the obsession with these cities, he wondered—the two friends systematically burgled seven apartments belonging to students. The next weekend he took his girlfriend out to a fancy dinner and the pair looked out over the Eternal City with its domes and rooftops lit like a theater set. Mimi's cheeks glowed with the wine and she smiled at him with her perfect California teeth. She was always so delighted with Rome that whenever he was with her he began to feel like a foreigner himself. From their perch on Monte Mario, Pietro saw his city anew.

That night when they returned to her apartment, she peeled off her clothes, flopped onto her bed, and gave him a bashful smile.

"Okay," she said. "Sono pronta."

"Per che cosa?" he asked.

"We can—," she giggled nervously. "You know."

"You know?" he repeated.

"Here," she said, gesturing to her ass.

It was true he had once asked her if he could have her there. He had been quite drunk that night and secretly happy she'd refused. He loved sleeping with Mimi, but he liked thinking of her as remaining innocent in some fashion.

"But I thought that was what you wanted." She looked at him. "Ho pensato … um. I mean, pensavo … I mean, I want you to."

"Ah, bella." And he lay down beside her, stroking her long blonde hair.

After Mimi left Rome in early December, Pietro felt hollowed out. To fill the void he and Bruno continued their game of hunting for American girls at clubs in Testaccio and bars in Trastevere then surreptitiously stealing their laptops or cellphones. That January he slept with a few students, but he never met any like Mimi and he knew he never would. As soon as he had stolen from that first apartment he had rendered himself unworthy of such a girl. Such a good girl. And oh, her long American legs and velvety skin.

It was Carnival when he ran into Francesca of the round ass and the propensity for blowjobs. His English had improved and he and Bruno had spent the better part of the evening chatting up girls who were sloppy drunk and teetering around wearing Venetian masks. But he hadn't been in the mood. It was the same club where he had met Mimi and even at the distance of a few months, he felt he had missed an opportunity. He had logged hours daydreaming—imagining himself living with her near the sea in San Diego, the two of them opening an Italian-style bakery. They had spoken a couple times after she left, but their conversations only created more distance between them.

"Non ti ricordi di me?" Francesca said. She was waitressing and held a fistful of empty mugs in one hand and a cigarette in the other.

"Macché?" he said. "Of course I remember you."

But the only way he could still his mind and keep from revisiting that first night and the memory of Mimi's laugh as she clung to him on the back of his Vespa was to pull Francesca into the bathroom and bend her over the sink. As he pushed up her dress, he noticed she had several new tattoos, the most prominent of which was a snake that wrapped around her hip and slithered over her back, the serpent's forked tongue pointing him lower and lower.

At first it had been a relief to only speak Italian again, but his time spent with Francesca only made him yearn more acutely for Mimi's pantomime and her laughter as she paused the conversation to consult her bilingual dictionary. True, Francesca always understood what Pietro said, but it soon became clear she would never understand him. Their time together had been nothing more than a tresca and he had not believed her when she told him she was pregnant.

"Maybe it isn't mine," Pietro said.

"They don't call it the oldest trick in the book for no reason," Bruno said.

Pietro had to admit he and Francesca had never once used a condom.

Her belly began to swell regardless of the fact that she continued to smoke an alarming number of cigarettes, even joints. She harangued him and called him and hassled him, and he was unsure how to extract himself. He thought about his mother and what she would have advised him to do. Then, in her third month, Francesca stopped smoking and claimed she had changed. And she wanted Pietro to change, too. But what would he change? And how? He had long since given up making deliveries for his aunt and when he had phoned her she said she couldn't help him, her boss would never hire him back. Pietro had quit showing up for his shifts when he and Bruno began 'working' together. He couldn't support a child by picking up girls and stealing their laptops. Or could he? Bruno advised him to get out now before the baby was born and it was too late. His friend could not understand his sense of obligation to Francesca. And frankly, neither could he. Francesca declared that he should—and would—move in with them.

"We're a family now," she insisted.

And part of him wanted that—a family. But not with Francesca. Still he dreamed of Mimi and their bakery in California. And, sometimes, when he was really feeling sorry for himself, he even thought about Maria Grazia.

Francesca Morelli shared a damp ground floor flat with her over-bearing mother Donatella. The place had little light and even less charm, but at least it brought him back into the center of Rome, away from the squalor of the periphery and his father whose drinking had become unbearable. The apartment was all the family had left of what had once been a converted shed or barn belonging to Francesca's great grandmother since the days when those narrow alleyways at the foot of the Janiculum hill were home to a patchwork of vegetable gardens and chicken coops that had sprung up alongside the convent that was later converted into the Regina Coeli jail. To name a jail after the Queen of Heaven struck Pietro as both blasphemous and purely Roman. But the sound of the lovers calling out to the inmates from up on the hill soothed him during quiet Sunday mornings when Francesca and her mother hunted flea market bargains for the baby at Porta Portese. Donatella and Francesca were proud to be among the few Trasteverini left in the area, which had gentrified around them and become artists' studios and galleries and chic attic apartments housing expats who cultivated bougainvillea on their terraces to block the view of the jail.

Pietro took a job in a nearby bakery. He preferred working nights. It helped avoid the issue of sleeping beside Francesca. Or sleeping with Francesca. Sundays were his only day free. His salary was a joke compared to what he had made off a stolen scooter or laptop and it hurt him immensely to bake someone else's desserts, but he found a certain dignity in earning his own way. His hands seemed to remember what his mind had blotted out and the simple act of dusting a rolling pin with flour made him believe he was on the right path. He was a grown up now. He would emulate the father Gianmarco had been when he was small, rather than the kind he had actually become.

Bruno would come round in the middle of the night after an evening out at the bars, knocking on the back door while Pietro was pressing dough in a pan or pulling pastries from the oven, and they would always end up getting high together. His friend tempted him with stories of his conquests and cajoled him with the thick wad of cash he always seemed to have in his pocket. Pietro quickly grew to resent the bakery and, in turn, his boss and the meager salary he paid. But he resented Francesca more—her swollen belly, the ink greening her skin, and the falsetto pitch of her voice that reminded him of a swarm of mosquitos buzzing around his head.

As he came to see it, his only choice was to continue selling hash. And to begin selling cocaine. After all, he had discovered a new clientele— American college students. So, in spite of Francesca's protests when he and Bruno went out in the evenings, the two continued trawling for Study Abroads, a task that had become even easier now that Pietro lived in Trastevere. The two friends would saunter over to Campo de' Fiori at an hour when the girls were sure to be well and drunk or station themselves at one of the pubs populating the area near the Ponte Sisto. And, if it happened that while selling drugs to the boys, Pietro also managed to sleep with the occasional girl, or somehow come across a purse with an iPhone or a tote bag with a Kindle inside, so be it.

Sophia Albescu wasn't anti-baby. She was anti-stroller. Baby carriages populated the foyer of her palazzo, each parked at a haphazard angle mimicking the way Italians carelessly abandoned their cars all over the city at the dinner hour. To add insult to injury, the administrator had decreed that bicycles were no longer allowed inside. This infuriated Sophia. Stealing bicycles was a Roman tradition—hers had disappeared the week before. But it wasn't just the bicycle situation. It was her dog Zeno. He loved babies and longed to nose up close to them, even lick them, tail wagging. But whenever she stepped off the elevator into the fray of strollers, she was forced to run the gauntlet of mothers, all cowering and clutching their infants as if Zeno were a pit bull with terrific jaws ready to sever a tiny bootie-clad foot.

Only Marcolino was allowed to pet him. Timid in every other way, the baby would come to life whenever he saw Zeno, reaching out of his stroller to tenderly stroke the big dog's muzzle. The child had angelic curls and wide brown eyes, like his father's though surely less bloodshot, Sophia had noticed. His cheeks were enormously pudgy— his whole body was pudgy, even his tiny fists—a fleshiness that bore no connection to the waif-like appearance of both his parents. The father was on something, for sure. He had the vacant look of those junkies panhandling for cash on the bridge. And anyone could see the young mother had an eating disorder. Sophia could never tell if the girl was depressed, high, or maybe just hungry. But something was off. With both of them.

Marcolino, on the other hand, was utter delight. Whenever he saw Zeno, he would burst into a smile and Sophia would make the dog sit so the baby could pet him. During these encounters, which happened in the street, the child's mother was most often smoking and weeping or shouting into her cellphone. In any other city this might have been awkward, but Romans had little issue with making a public scene. To Sophia it had always seemed that the larger the audience, the more theatrical things became. On the other hand, if the father was pushing the stroller—the pair was never together—he would crouch down beside Zeno, take his child's hand, and help him pet the dog's ears. The guy gave her the creeps, but he sure seemed to love his son.

Sophia did not chat with her neighbors if she could help it. Zeno and the stroller-faction had put her at odds with most of them from the start. In truth, she disliked Italians, although she had lived among them for years. The minute they heard her accent their attitude instantly changed. Of all the people who knew her, Salvatore seemed to be the only one who never realized Sophia was Moldavian—which to Italians ranked somewhere below the Albanians, and even the Romanians, but somewhere above the Bangladeshis and Africans, all of whom occupied a collective rung beneath the Filipinos, who were "at the very least Catholic" as her employer had once explained to her.

Salvatore had seen her security badge for the university and noticed she always carried a book with her wherever she went—her bus rides to and from work were interminable—and had inferred that she was a professor. She did work at a university, but cleaning classrooms and offices during the early morning hours. And she babysat afternoons and Friday evenings for a wealthy French-Italian family in the Vigna Clara district of Rome. She had met Salvatore—and Zeno—when taking the family's aging Jack Russell to the vet to have him put down. After the deed was done, Sophia sat in the waiting room and cried, in part because she was so angry they had insisted she be the one to escort poor Jacques to his end.

"Poverina," Salvatore said. He offered her a tissue and put his hand on her knee to comfort her, having assumed the dog was hers. She never corrected his mistake. And later she sang the dead dog's praises for putting her in Salvatore's path.

Aside from her native tongue and Russian, Sophia also spoke French, so she had learned Italian easily. She tried to cultivate the air of expatriate rather than immigrant. She had changed her first name and modeled herself after her employer who was exacting about how she cared for and fed the two children, yet generous when it came to her wardrobe, sometimes even giving her shoes and purses as hand-me-downs. Chloè DeAngelis had a shopping problem and she didn't want her husband Enrico to find out about it. The signora had grown bored being the wife of a restaurant owner. Michelin star or no, her husband was never home, so she passed her days in the boutiques near Piazza di Spagna, rapidly rotating outfits in and out of her armoire and pressing designer shopping bags into Sophia's hands before she left for the bus stop.

Sophia and Salvatore had been seeing one another for several months, when the issue of Zeno came up. Whenever they met, he picked her up in his BMW at some appointed spot and brought her to what he referred to as his garçonnière. He claimed he had lived in the apartment when he was a student and could never bring himself to give it up. She didn't believe he'd ever lived there—he hadn't even furnished it with appliances until she moved in. She imagined he'd brought dozens of women there, but it didn't bother her. She could never fall for Salvatore, much less any Italian, but definitely not Salvatore. He was forever snarling orders at someone on the other end of the phone, he dripped sweat over her in bed, and he had stubby fingers. Still, the idea of her encounters with him made her feel sophisticated, if only for a few hours a month.

For years she had lived with the nuns, renting a room in their convent to save money. Any extra earned she sent to her aging parents and sickly brother whom she was rarely able to visit. If she didn't have to pay rent she could finally afford to travel home. So, if taking Zeno meant acquiring the apartment rent free, even if it meant seeing Salvatore more often or accommodating any fetish he might have, she could accept those conditions. For the attic was a dream. And anyway, she had thought, once she lived there, she could always change the locks. Everybody knew it was nearly impossible to evict a tenant in Italy.

The piccolo Marco—Marcolino—was born a month early by C-section. Donatella helped her daughter Francesca waddle to the emergency room at Santo Spirito after her water broke unexpectedly. It had been an unseasonably cold and rainy autumn night and not a taxi was to be found. They had considered the bus, but a bus would only crisscross the bridges of the Tiber and take longer than walking, so they carried on alongside the river. Donatella was not pleased about having a grandchild. She recalled her own trip to the hospital just over two decades earlier. She was only forty-three, but she knew no man wanted to date a grandmother.

Rather than clutching her belly, Francesca had a death-grip on her iPhone for the entire walk. "He promised he would be here."

Her mother looked at her watch, lit a cigarette, and said nothing. Both women had tried repeatedly to reach Pietro, but the calls went straight to voice mail.

Pietro had grown distant, moody. He was rarely home. Francesca suspected he had another girlfriend, but he denied it. They had argued bitterly for most of her pregnancy. Now that they were a couple he didn't like the fact that she had been with so many men. And she was jealous he spent his evenings out, rarely accounting for his time. Whenever she asked him to take her along, he accused her of having trapped him, still claiming he didn't believe he was the baby's father. No matter how many times she explained she had used contraceptives, he refused to accept the facts. It was true she'd been erratic taking her pills, missing nearly a dozen that first month. Still, she never imagined she could get pregnant so easily. And an abortion had been out of the question.

Nonetheless, the child's paternity was effortlessly confirmed when he was born. Baby fat aside, Marcolino resembled Pietro in nearly every way. This rankled Francesca. Whenever anyone peeped into the carriage, they commented that he didn't take after her in the least. It was as if her DNA had been erased.

When she first returned home from the hospital, she breast-fed Marcolino and felt blissed out with a kind of hormone-induced wonder at her tiny son. However, the process grew more and more difficult. Her breasts were enormous and ached continuously. She dripped milk whenever the infant cried, even for a second, staining her clothing. When she woke in the middle of the night to feed him, she could never fall back asleep. She found drinking a couple glasses of wine and smoking a joint was the only thing that helped. Six weeks on, she went back to smoking cigarettes to lose weight. She had never been thin, but after the delivery whenever she looked in the mirror all she saw were the extra kilos gained from her pregnancy and the jagged red scar from her surgery. She was only twenty-one and she felt past her prime. She began to miss her old life, the attention she got from men working nights at the club. The business of the baby was monotonous. Donatella helped her when she could, but more often than not her mother did double shifts dispensing cigarettes and lottery tickets at the Tabacchi around the corner.

That spring and summer it seemed to rain and rain and it was always such a production to get the baby carriage on the little electric bus or even to push it along the cobblestones of Via della Lungara. It made no sense bringing Marcolino to the playground in the piazza— he was still too small—but sometimes Francesca went anyway. And she was always disappointed when she did. All the other mothers were so old, she thought. So many were in their thirties. Or even older. She stared at a mother with twins about the same age as Marcolino. The woman had let her hair go gray and must have been at least forty.

"Che schifo," Francesca thought, repulsed.

She immediately pointed Marcolino's stroller out of the square and bumped along the narrow streets toward the tattoo parlor on Via del Moro.

"Aò," the tattoo artist said. "Guarda chi c'è."

"Here," she said, pulling the neck of her sweater over her shoulder to expose her collarbone.

He moved in a little closer and ran his fingers over the area she had pointed to, seeming to brush against her breast intentionally.

Francesca tugged her top over her head, then smoothed her hair.

"Do I need to take off my bra?" she asked.

"It wouldn't hurt," he said.

On the baby's first birthday, Pietro baked a torta della nonna in honor of his mother, and invited his father and Aunt Giovanna to help celebrate. His family made Francesca nervous, but now that Marcolino was getting bigger she hoped they could all get along. Just the fact that they would spend the baby's birthday together was a good sign, she thought. But Pietro grew sullen when his father never materialized. Gianmarco had only met his grandson once, just two weeks after he was born. Giovanna arrived toting an enormous package: a high chair for the baby. Donatella was irritated by the expensive gift. She had bought practical clothing— bibs and onesies from the nearby market stalls—that now looked cheap in comparison. The two women made strained small talk, which grew less strained as they finished off the prosecco. Pietro smoked incessantly. He repeatedly picked up his cellphone, stared at it, and put it back down again. Francesca got drunk and flirted with Bruno. She had never noticed he was so good looking. Bruno got drunk and flirted with Francesca. She'd lost a ton of weight, he thought, but her tits were still huge. Pietro left without saying a word and didn't return for over an hour and when he did, he disappeared in the bathroom and it sounded like he was vomiting. By the time they lit the candle on Marcolino's cake, the child had long been asleep in his new high chair.

Along with the winter chill, the holidays arrived, but they didn't bother inviting anyone over and there was little cheer in the air. Their neighborhood had emptied out, most Romans having left town to spend time with relatives. By day, only the gypsies waiting to visit relatives in jail populated the café on the corner. By night, the streets were nearly deserted. Christmas was a disappointment—they had snorted lines and watched television in their dark apartment while Marcolino cried in his crib. That evening, Pietro had slipped out when Francesca was in the bathroom. She was livid. Worse, she was bored. She scrolled through the numbers on her cell phone and sent text messages to a few old boyfriends, but none responded.

Just after New Year, she dressed the baby in his best outfit for the Befana, but it was she who had had an epiphany. She opened her closet, tugging all her favorite clothing down from the hangers, flinging miniskirts and dresses on the bed. She stripped off her leggings and sweatshirt and began to try everything on. Her pre-pregnancy clothes were no longer too small, but actually too big. It was time to show off her new figure to her old friends from work. She straightened her hair and carefully applied thick strokes of black eyeliner, lots of mascara. She put a knit cap on Marcolino and wrapped him in his pale blue blanket. As they made their way down the street, she stopped to let him pet the big red dog that some neighbor's housekeeper always seemed to be walking. Romanian trash, Francesca thought, looking at the woman. But the dog was nice. He loved Marcolino.

When she arrived at the club it was still early. Only Antonio was there, slicing lemons and setting up the bar. "Che bel bambino," he said, but he wasn't admiring the baby, he was staring at Francesca. Actually, he was staring at Francesca's cleavage. She wore a short tight dress with a plunging neckline and tall stiletto-heeled boots. They had hooked up a few times when she worked there, usually after he'd had an argument with his girlfriend.

He put two shots of rum on the bar and glanced again at the baby.

"A toast to—"

"—Marcolino," she reminded him.

"No," he said. "To you."

A mojito and three shots later, Francesca found herself on her knees behind the bar, unzipping Antonio's jeans.

"I've never fucked a woman who had a baby before," he said.

Of course, as luck would have it, by the time the club had filled up and she was stumbling back to the bus stop, she discovered several frantic messages from Pietro, but she knew better than to call him when she was drunk. They would only argue. She prayed he wouldn't be there when she got home. She switched off her phone. She would say the battery had run out. She waited another forty minutes before the bus finally arrived and was dismayed to see it so crowded. She struggled to lift the stroller on board. Francesca hated riding the night bus. It was always full of Vu Cumprà—African street vendors toting designer knock-offs and those Asian guys who sold the roses. She didn't like sitting beside foreigners. The bus lurched along Via Marmorata and she nearly nodded off in her seat. Marcolino stared up at her with wide eyes.

When they finally arrived at her stop, she snapped awake, and hurried across the Ponte Mazzini, the bridge nearest home. But she found the house empty. There was a note from her mother. Pietro's father had died of a heart attack and he had gone to the morgue, but there was some confusion about which one. There were no other details. Francesca spilled the contents of her purse and diaper bag out on the table and began sifting through the clutter. She needed a cigarette, but must have forgotten hers on the bar. Marcolino began to cry.

"Fuck," she said.

No one had seen Pietro Pietrini for days. He did not attend the mass for his father, but he arrived at the cemetery in time for the burial. To the few people gathered there, he looked strung out, frantic. He had a deep gash across his right cheek and the shadow of a bruise forming beneath the eye. As they stood in the bitter cold, Pietro restlessly shifted from foot to foot and stared at the headstone that bore his parents' names. He had not once visited Giuseppina's grave. As they lowered Gianmarco's coffin into the earth, he held onto his son's tiny hand. Marcolino was just learning to walk and was very fond of toddling off. Afterward, they were invited back to his Aunt Giovanna's where they all had their share of wine and grappa. By the time they got home, Pietro was a bit drunk and less on edge. He gave Marcolino his bath and carried him into the bedroom to his crib.

"You deserve better than me," he said.

"I know," Francesca blurted out from the kitchen.

"No," he said. "The baby."

Donatella smirked and lit a cigarette.

Francesca did the same. "What happened to your face?" she asked, finally.

"Nothing," he said.

Like his father before him, Pietro owed money to the wrong man. He had dodged his supplier for weeks, but after identifying his father's body he'd been desperate to get high and had actually called Vincenzo himself. A mistake. But the following morning, Pietro announced he wasn't going to do any more drugs and that he was finished dealing. He knew he had debts, but he would just have to take care of them one by one. He would go back to working in a bakery.

"Why bother?" Francesca said. She didn't look up from the text message she was sending.

He drove his Vespa all over the city in the January cold and was soon reminded that Rome was not the easiest place to find a job, not even an underpaid one. He filled out applications and knocked on doors. He asked favors of people he had known since he was young. He even tried the bakery where he had worked before Marcolino was born.

"No," his former boss told him. "We hired an indiano and he costs half what we paid you."

By chance, Pietro saw a sign in a shop window near the Vatican. The owner, a woman, needed a hand for the next couple months. And she would pay him in cash.

"It will get busy before Lent," she explained, "but after Easter it drops off."

"Right," Pietro said. "No problem."

As he stood at the metal counter running the mixer, the heat from the ovens was intolerable. He had a constant headache. Without the coke, he felt tired. Without the joints, he felt jittery. The more he thought about all the money he owed, the more anxious he became. He kept his phone turned off to avoid Vincenzo. Even Bruno. He wanted to stick with it, though, and accepted as many hours as the signora offered. She was about the age Giuseppina would have been and her gentle manner reminded him of his mother, which only made him feel worse.

That Friday afternoon it had rained most of the day and the rain had turned to sleet alternating with snow. The forecast announced an enormous storm. The signora closed early and Pietro began making his way back to Trastevere on his Vespa. He was soaked before he'd even covered a couple of blocks. Just before the tunnel, the traffic shuddered and sloshed to a halt, and he glanced over at the Via della Conciliazione. Anyone who could manage to was leaving work early, but the tourists were as indomitable as the Bangladeshi umbrella sellers. Sleet pelted the famous square, cheap black umbrellas rippled in the gusts and the façade of the Vatican seemed almost to withdraw into the distance, all but enshrouded by white.

Ignoring the forecast, Francesca had gone out with Antonio. It was the second time that week. A few days earlier he had come home to find Antonio on the sofa playing with Marcolino and Francesca prancing around in a black mesh dress, cut low in the back, the better to display her tattoos. "Your turn," she had said, slamming the door behind them. But somehow, he hadn't anticipated a repeat.

"How long did you expect her to wait for you?" Donatella asked.

He knew she was right. He hadn't been fair to her daughter, but that didn't make him like Francesca any better. In fact, he was fairly certain he hated her. She was a terrible mother. And he was, he knew, an even worse father. He had never wanted any of this.

"Maybe you should think about getting your own place," Donatella said.

It was so typical of her to make decisions for everybody else, he thought. Then again, it was her house. What was he going to do? Live with Francesca while she slept with Antonio? And how many others would come after him? He had been avoiding his Aunt Giovanna who had asked him to help clean out his father's apartment. He wondered if the locks had already been changed. He tried to imagine Marcolino living in that squalor, much less himself. He couldn't go back there. Not even if he wanted to. And his Aunt's new husband was hardly going to let him stay with them, much less offer to help with childcare. It was clear he had wanted nothing to do with any of them after the funeral.

He found the baby's coat and put it on him.

"Where are you going?"

"For a walk."

"It's too cold out."

"He's my son," Pietro said. "Not yours."

"Now you want to be a father," she said.

He needed air. He needed to think. Sometimes he would take Marcolino down to the river and they would feed the ducks. It was almost as if his son smiled with his entire body whenever he saw them. Marcolino loved dogs and he loved ducks. But he was terrified of the seagulls with their enormous wings and their almost human shrieking as they dipped down to the surface of the Tiber to scavenge and scoop up whatever they could.

"Non ti preoccupare," he told him. He explained there wouldn't be any seagulls now, but the child didn't look worried. It was Pietro who was in a panic. He fumbled with the stroller and gave up, carrying his son out into the street. The cobblestones were dark and slick with rain. Deep puddles had formed and the snow had begun to accumulate in frothy patches. He frowned up at the sky. It was too cold to be outside. Marcolino squirmed. He wanted to be put down, but it was too slippery. Pietro's phone rang and he shifted his son to his hip and answered without looking to see who had called.

"Finally," Bruno said.

"Francesca has a boyfriend."

"Sounds like you need a drink."

"And Vincenzo is looking for me," Pietro said.

"Maybe something stronger."

"Whatever you can get."

"Ci penso io," Bruno told him.

Donatella had her head in the refrigerator when Pietro opened the door.

"Back so soon?" she asked. He handed off Marcolino to her and left without answering.

He put on his helmet and found the winter gloves he kept in the little trunk of his Vespa. As he put them on, he remembered they were the pair Maria Grazia had given him just three years earlier. The realization made him feel ill. He wrenched off the gloves and threw them on the ground. He lit a cigarette and inhaled as deeply as possible, but smoking was not going to do the trick. It was so cold he had to kick-start his scooter. The motor sputtered as he put it into gear and drove down the darkened street. Large wet snowflakes twirled in the light from his headlamp, exploding against the windshield and skittering like teardrops over the glass before hitting him in the face. The thought of leaving Francesca with his son—much less Francesca and another man—filled Pietro with an unfamiliar rage.

On a late afternoon in early February, Salvatore Scaduto visited his mistress Sophia. It had been several weeks since they had spent any time together and he missed her—she always smelled of sandalwood and welcomed him wearing something serious and studious, yet sexy—but he missed his dog, Zeno, more. The summer before, his wife Nella claimed she'd developed a sudden allergy to Zeno and insisted he get rid of him. For the entire season she had dabbed her eyes with a handkerchief or exaggeratedly blown her nose whenever the hound came near. At first, Salvatore believed it was the acacia trees blooming in their neighborhood. Eventually, though, he felt certain that Nella was simply punishing him. She had wanted to spend the entire summer in Argentario, but he had promised their house to a business associate for the week of Ferragosto and she was furious. He had mended the situation by booking a trip to Zanzibar for the following winter, but she was relentless in her persecution of the dog. Salvatore simply could not bring himself to give up Zeno—he loved him and he loved having an excuse to go out on long after-dinner walks, leaving his wife and daughters behind—but the discussion had grown heated and exasperating and, finally, intolerable.

"I adore dogs," Sophia had explained. And she would happily have taken Zeno, but only small dogs were allowed in the apartment she rented.

Salvatore had had mixed feelings about giving his dog to a mistress. It would surely complicate things. But whenever he looked at Zeno he could not imagine to whom else he might entrust him, or worse, never seeing him again. And so it happened that Sophia became Zeno's caretaker and the large dog lived with her in her tiny attic flat near the botanic garden in Trastevere. Of course, Salvatore had supplied her with the apartment. But he didn't mind. He had brought his lovers there for years, having bought it at auction for a song. Some day he would reclaim it for one of his daughters, but until then, if it meant Zeno was well cared for, Sophia could have it. And he liked the idea of "keeping" her. It would have been crass to charge her rent, but it excited him to think she would always feel indebted to him. Actually, she had made great improvements to the place since she arrived, and she took excellent care of his Zeno. Not to mention his cock.

He had never asked Sophia why she had no family of her own. He only knew she was a professor of some sort and spoke several languages. Her Italian was fluent, but her accent instantly marked her as foreign. She had explained it to him once, her complicated lineage, but he'd since forgotten. What interested him was the pale softness of her white skin, her full lips. He had never had a better blowjob in his life. For Salvatore, Sophia was a revelation. He'd slept with plenty women, but none quite like her. She never complained, never asked for explanations when he canceled, never lobbied for more of his time or for him to take her away for the weekend. In fact, she demanded nothing and in return he gave her more than he might have ever imagined. Whenever Salvatore had an errand that would bring him downtown or require him to drive along the river, he would send Sophia a text message. He rarely remembered a moment when she was not available to him and yet he knew she led a busy life. Just the sound of her "Bonjour, Bèbè" as she opened the door would make him want to fuck her immediately, sometimes slowly, sometimes quickly, but whichever it was, he always left himself time to walk Zeno before he had to go, sending the dog back up in the elevator to her before hopping in his BMW and racing off.

On the eve of the snowstorm, though, things had gone differently. A bitter rain had been falling when he'd arrived and by the time he and Sophia finished making love—he still called it that, he was, after all, Italian—the rain had turned to icy sleet speckled with wet heavy snowflakes. He took Zeno out, anyway, and walked him up the steps and onto the bridge where he noticed the dome of St. Peter's visible through the bare branches of the tall trees along the river. He continued on toward Via Giulia, the dog stepping over puddles as they went. Even at that hour, he found himself alone in the city, for all the

Romans had left work at lunch time, hurrying to their homes before the weather worsened, and only tourists photographed those first early flakes fluttering over the city, dusting the Arch of Constantine and drifting down through the oculus of the Pantheon. But Salvatore was as content as he had ever been, Sophia had more than taken care of him—she had the body of a thirty-year-old, yet he was certain she must have been at least forty—and his faithful Zeno was by his side.

As he walked in the snow he decided he would take his family skiing in the Abruzzo the following weekend. And as soon as his wife crossed his mind, his phone rang. Nella calling to say the flight home from visiting her parents in Milan had been canceled. "What a shame," he said, claiming he had booked their favorite restaurant for her return. "I'll call Enrico and cancel." Taking advantage of not having to pick up his wife and daughters at Fiumicino, Salvatore made his way back to the apartment where he carefully toweled dry the dog, rubbing his ruffled spine lovingly. He filled Zeno's metal bowls with his favorite food and fresh water. Then he quickly led Sophia back to the bed where they remained as the snow began to collect in small drifts against the French doors to the terrace.

He spent hours making love to her and was quite impressed with himself for how many times he had managed to bring them both to a climax—having only planned a quickie, he hadn't even thought to bring Viagra, but then, with Sophia, what man would need such a thing? He and Nella still slept in the same bed, but they never had sex. It had taken so much effort to have children—and so much medical intervention—that any intimacy they might have shared when they were first married had been crushed by the fertility process.

Salvatore had never spent an entire night with Sophia and as he lay in bed beside her in the apartment he owned he felt a sense of propriety over her, as well. The snow fell silently beyond the tall panes of glass and covered the skylight above them and it was as if he had been transported from Rome to the French Alps. No. Saint Petersburg.

Yes, that was it, Russia. And Sophia was his fair mistress. Aside from Zeno's soft snores, everything felt foreign. To sleep beside a woman he was enormously attracted to. To see snow falling and falling in the Roman sky beyond the windowsills that had once been his, but were now shrouded in sheer white curtains and home to small white orchids in small white vases. All was white and wonderful. The sheets and Sophia's pale skin and he drifted, like snow, in and out of strange dreams.

When he woke, the sun was hard and glittery, the room achingly bright. Zeno slept beside him on the bed and Sophia stood at the stove in a white silk robe. She struck a match, lighting the low blue flame and putting the espresso on. He drank his coffee in a rush, slipping on his shoes so he could take Zeno for a walk in the snow. Salvatore felt a childish excitement when he stepped outside into the deep snow. There he found only one set of tracks near the door, he could not tell from which direction the footprints had come or gone—if the person had left just ahead of him or recently returned. Zeno leapt into the whiteness with joy, rolled in the snow, then shook himself clean, bouncing up in the air in front of his master and nipping at the edge of the leash.

That morning, Salvatore Scaduto struggled to get Zeno away from the river's edge and back up the endless flight of steps from the embankment. Not a single car passed. He stood in the snow on the corner, pulling his cell phone from the breast pocket of his cashmere coat. He blocked his Caller ID and dialed 112 to report what he had seen on the bridge or rather what he had not seen: a baby—a toddler—tossed into the Tiber like a piece of trash. He clutched the phone with one frozen hand and clutched the leash in the other. The dog lunged with all his strength back toward the river, howling a terrible moaning howl the entire time he was on the phone.

He glanced back at the desolate snow-covered bridge then across at the Regina Coeli jail that loomed up out of the cold air and from behind whose barred windows it was impossible to know who else might have observed the incident or who might be observing him now. He would not wait for the police. He could not risk getting involved. Nella might find out about Zeno. In the distance, sirens were already approaching. He hustled his agitated dog back through the snow, rang his mistress's phone once, hung up, and sent the animal up to her in the elevator.

It was the following weekend, in the ski lodge at Campo Felice, when Salvatore read *La Repubblica*'s account of the drowned infant Marcolino. And it was only then, seeing the photos that he recognized the boy, the baker's son, who had arrived at his office on a rickety moped and pleaded with him on behalf of his father to keep the family business. He remembered the way he had laughed and brushed off the kid without so much as a thought. His father had owed him money for years. Plain and simple. Besides, Salvatore couldn't wait to get his hands on that property. He knew he would make a killing on the apartment and the bakery when he sold them. And he had.

Pura Goa Lawah

It was on the road to Denpasar to renew her visa when she'd landed upon it. The driver Putu had just swerved around a scooter—three kids perched upon it and leaning—then veered toward the shoulder where a woman with bare feet and a hiked-up sarong crouched, jabbing a stick at a burning plastic bag. Smoke snaking through the open windows of the vehicle. Her morning dose of jamu sloshing in her stomach, telltale wave of the motion sickness that plagued her.

Stare straight, she reminded herself.

Eyes on the horizon.

But there was no horizon, only a knot of traffic as they slowed to a crawl for the tail end of a passing procession making its way into a walled temple, its guardian statues resembling fierce cartoons. Gamelan music jangling her already jangled nerves.

Focus.

Find your drishti.

That's right, she thought.

Drishti.

It was so perfect, really.

She clutched her newly returned passport ever tighter for fear of it flapping open to reveal her true name. Over the years she had made varied attempts at inhabiting other monikers. None had lasted. None had ever been capable of erasing the name her father had seen fit to saddle her with. But now, as if the new moon were delivering her from it, she rechristened herself Drishti. Right there. In the minivan. Silently repeating it over and over, even though she wanted to shout it. With a calm befitting her new identity, she vowed to embody concentration, and focused her line of vision over Putu's dashboard idols and out to the road.

Drishti sat sandwiched between two others in the row just behind the driver. On her left was a woman with over-processed yellow wisps artfully swept upward in a plastic clip in hopes of disguising the bald patches peeping between strands. She had already noted the woman's chipped pink polish, the freckled sag of her cleavage, and her sequined flip-flops that morning in the Bintang parking lot where a loose constellation of tourists, expats, and overstays stood waiting for the driver. In one fashion or another, each had found the same woman, also named Putu, who facilitated tourist visas from the stoop of a small shop off Jalan Hanoman. Ten days earlier, Drishti had forked over 700 rupiah and her American passport with some trepidation to this stranger who demonstrated no official documentation and offered no guarantees, instructing her to wait for a text message.

The passenger beside her—it was now clear she was Australian—spoke over her to the lanky man on Drishti's right. The man's jaw hosted the shadow of a reddish beard, his large hands cupping the worn knees of what her father would have called dungarees in a shade of denim that screamed 70s. Not in a hipster sort of way, but plucked from a pile of donated clothing at the Salvation Army sort of way. The man had been quiet at first, but after the Aussie embraced the role of interlocutor, he began to grow more animated, commandeering the conversation.

Once upon a time he'd been a UPS deliveryman, but a busted knee and an expired insurance plan had put him out of the business. He'd lost everything. Or whatever there was for losing, he said, which included a tract house in a subdivision outside Salt Lake and a beloved Fat Boy, neither of which he'd come close to paying off. He introduced himself. Not to Drishti, but he wasn't exactly ignoring her either. His name was Kenneth Love Billings. He said God had brought him to Bali and announced that he was a Spiritual Advisor. He assured whoever was listening—and by now everyone else in the van, even those in the way back, had an ear cocked his way—that he administered consultations on Monday nights at the back table of a Penestanan cafe on a first come, first serve basis.

He did not charge, he told them. But he felt it only right to accept donations, the suggested amount being, "Fifty US."

He added that he owned no phone.

"Email?" the Aussie probed.

In response, Kenneth Love Billings hurled his long frame forward with a jerk and extracted a small stack of cards from his pocket, dispensing them all around. Hands reached up from behind her to take them. Not wanting to seem impolite, Drishti accepted one, tucking it into her passport as if it were a bookmark. If she'd ever envisaged a spiritual advisor—and she had—the ones she'd imagined looked nothing like Kenneth Love Billings. Yet not having conjured his likeness did not diminish the fact that she yearned for—something. Call it a guru. Maybe just a teacher. Anyone who could help her navigate her way back out of the many forked paths of the rice paddies and into the beyond.

Since her arrival, she'd faithfully attended Yoga Nidra classes at sundown, though she usually fell asleep, what with the delicious weight of Kintamani black sand inside the hand-stitched eye pillows and the instructor's silky voice guiding her through the meditation. She had also tested out healing massages, vitamin B12 shots, and Sacred Colonics. She'd even submitted to rectal ozone injections, allowing the practitioner to see what only her ex-husband had ever viewed up close. And now she was waitlisted for a session with a Life Coach who would administer beta release therapy to align the left and right sides of her brain. Assuming she would get her visa renewal approved.

But a Life Coach wasn't necessarily spiritual, she thought. Years ago that word might have made her shudder. No more. Like everyone else on the island, she had read the book and watched the movie, but would never acknowledge a desire to emulate it. Visiting a shaman had become passé. And everybody knew the shaman had long since lost his powers when he sold himself out to publish a coffee table book. Or so she'd been told, quickly omitting that stop from her itinerary. Not entirely without regret.

She liked to think of herself as a traveler—not a tourist—and she found it bothersome that she was not alone in this. Aside from the mother-daughter foodie duo she'd met in Seminyak and the brunette from the Bay Area who'd gloated about hooking up with a Kuta Cowboy, every person Drishti encountered felt the same way. Nobody could admit a dependence on TripAdvisor or the fact they'd never actually eaten in a traditional warung. Nobody ever mentioned that their contact with the locals was limited to ordering overpriced raw food or making arrangements for spa days.

Disembodied voices—Goddess Girl, the Pregnant Swede, the Reflexologist with the shaved head, or maybe even the Standoffish Writer—chimed in from the back of the van. All with questions for Kenneth Love Billings. Drishti's motion sickness kept her from observing him more closely, something she very much wanted to do. She reminded herself to keep looking forward. Riding shotgun was a 20-something with a man bun. Batik tank and flowy white trousers. When he leaned over to pluck his iPhone—the ring tone playing Krishna Das—from the expedition grade daypack beside his tanned feet, she glimpsed the edges of a massive tattoo arcing up over his sculpted deltoids. Angel wings. A detail she'd missed when they chatted back at Bintang.

He had referred to himself as a Digital Nomad, a label she was unfamiliar with. But like so many of the other westerners in town, he'd mentioned completing his 500-hour yoga teacher training, although he was currently "consulting for Snapchat." For the next few minutes, Man Bun's phone conversation squelched the clamor for spiritual advice inside the van. Piecing together one-sided conversations was something of a specialty for Drishti. The last year of her marriage spent straining to eavesdrop on Stewart's calls had polished her ability to fill in blanks. From what she could glean, Man Bun had leased a house with a pool on the cheap from a Balinese family and was now advertising it on Airbnb for quadruple the price, the proceeds all neatly wired into his PayPal account while he crashed elsewhere.

As soon as he'd hung up, the phone rang again—Om Nayah Shivaya—and he made arrangements to surf Uluwatu the following day.

"YOLO," he said, tilting his body out of the window, not unlike a Labrador loving the breeze.

Although Putu The Visa Go Between had entrusted their fates to Putu The Driver, whatever bureaucratic magic she wielded resulted in the group of them skipping the haphazard line spilling onto the steps at Immigration. They were invited to sit in a crowded room with a sticky floor and little air. A crying baby and garbled announcements over a loud speaker created a din. Every so often a number flashed on the screen over the filthy window where nobody sat at the counter, and a few minutes later, the door beside it opened to reveal an officer who'd beckon the next person into the office for fingerprinting.

The process was brief and painless.

Or maybe it actually took a long time.

Had she simply tuned out? Even with her newfound focus, Drishti wasn't sure. She felt an extraordinary calm. Could it be the presence of Kenneth Love Billings on the folding chair beside her?

By day it was only the sounds of other travelers gathered at the community table to eat breakfast or passing along the path below her windows before venturing out. Nighttime was noisy. Not in the way cities are noisy, but much worse. It felt like being tested. Hazed, almost. She hadn't allowed herself a bungalow with air conditioning—she wanted to live the life or as close as she could get to it—and this meant renting a place with open-air architecture, bamboo beams stretching from the tops of the walls into the angle of the roof.

She often lay awake listening to the atonal chiming of gamelan from the village temple, which she found both disturbing and mesmerizing. And when there was no ceremony, the crescendo of crickets and ducks and frogs in the rice paddies took over. Who knew frogs could attain such decibels, she thought. Their croaking was operatic and, like everything else here, attuned to the phases of the moon. There was nothing charming about it, but at least the racket didn't continue all night.

Not so the roosters.

She'd long understood that crowing signaled daybreak. Turns out that was the stuff of myth. The roosters crowed and crowed and crowed, all night long, whether from rebellion or frenzied anticipation, one couldn't be sure. Perhaps for a rooster, first light was something akin to those cocktail napkins that say, "It's 5 o'clock somewhere." She decided she had been a city dweller so long the natural world had grown unfamiliar. In truth, she'd never really known nature at all. There was a single summer at sleep-away camp in the Poconos when she was nine, the time she embarrassed herself by falling off her horse. Pony, actually. She had never even owned a dog until she married Stewart. She missed the dog perhaps even more than she missed Stewart. But she had ceased to miss the trappings of their shared life. Everything here was stripped to essentials. She clung to the hope that this would bring her a sense of harmony, but she often found herself at odds with the realness of it all.

Her apartment had a resident gecko. Or maybe there were several. She preferred the idea of containment, convincing herself that it was the same miniscule lizard slithering away whenever she snapped on the bathroom light. But even if there were many more, she'd already proven to herself she could handle the small ones. It was the massive spotted geckos that alarmed her. That sinister "Ah-aow, Ah-aow" mating call reverberating from somewhere in the dark close by her bed. She feared one lived behind the painting hanging above her bedside table. She had made the mistake of reading up on them—they were called Tokays and could grow as long as 15 inches, and their jaws locked tight enough to snap off a finger. But that wasn't the worst of it.

There were also bats.

It wasn't the threat of dengue that kept her captive under her mosquito net, but the bats. Each night fruit bats visited the trees nearby then flew and flapped and rustled about her veranda. In the morning she'd wake to a gooey purplish puddle outside her door. Bat shit. And a lot of it. So much so she worried she might go a little bit bat shit herself. After slipping in the goop her first day she'd screamed, but immediately set about wiping up the mess. Nyoman later scolded her for cleaning and told her it wasn't shit after all.

"Lawah," she'd said. "Bats." She leaned on her broom, laughing and making spitting gestures to explain how they gorged themselves in nearby fruit trees, spitting out the skins and seeds onto the floor.

Afterward Drishti tried putting down newspaper in their preferred spot before going to bed. She knew she had OCD tendencies, but it wasn't just that. Why should poor Nyoman contend with such a mess when Drishti could simply fold the pages into the trash and stop skirting around the puddle with her mug of tea each morning? But the bats were clever, dribbling and expelling dark splotches just beside the newspaper, never on it, sometimes in a new places altogether. Yet, never on the furniture. Nyoman had laughed at her attempt to outwit them. There was no such thing as paper-training bats.

The night she returned from the visa run in Denpasar, a bat flew into her bedroom. She wanted to think of it as a good sign and tried to channel her inner Drishti, but she cowered beneath the flimsy mesh fabric tented over her bed and wept. The winged creature banged into the sliding glass doors and windows. She pulled the sheets over her head and listened. All grew quiet but every so often she heard the whisper of wings, like a book left open, its pages fluttering in the wind each time the bat flew close to her. Several minutes passed before she could accept that it was not going to find a way back out. She cried harder. She was ashamed; she knew it was just a tiny frightened thing. The bat continued to skitter helplessly about the room, colliding into the ceiling fan that, mercifully, was not switched on.

"Enough," she said, sniffling into her pillow.

Then, almost without realizing what she was doing, Drishti slipped off the pillowcase and tied it like a kerchief over her head. She steadied herself, inhaling and exhaling through her nose as if she were in yoga class, and removed the clothespins from the mosquito netting, slipping out from beneath it, rushing in her bare feet to shove open the windows and the tall glass doors.

And the bat passed over her as if it were a shadow.

She wasn't sure the beta alignment had really worked. Someone suggested getting her chakras balanced, but she felt she needed a break from treatments. Having shunned being a tourist resulted in not having seen much of the island or even the town. She had peeked into the main temple on Jalan Raya Ubud the day after she arrived and once visited the "art market" where, alongside versions of the same three or four print dresses she had seen all the other foreign women wearing, you could buy knickknacks and cheap luggage or fake Havaianas and T-shirts emblazoned with Ganesha. Over breakfast, Nyoman's husband Ketut had told her if she got up early enough, it would be worth visiting the morning market where the locals sold fruits and vegetables, and fresh spices. Drishti wanted to experience authenticity, but that notion was blighted by the beginning of her journey when she'd been demoralized at the first market she encountered on the island. That one was a little bit too local, she thought.

She recalled the unfamiliar smells, the stench really, the slimy black frogs in a rattan basket, the flies buzzing and landing on unrecognizable organs and meats, all bleeding onto the table as a man sliced away with a rusty blade. But that had turned out to be nothing compared to the desiccated rat the woman pulled dripping from a cylindrical blue cooler, waving its rigid body with its brittle little paws at her. Splashes of rat water grazing her cheek. Drishti's knees had buckled and she vomited into the mud. She reminded herself that she had not yet been Drishti at that time. She was someone else. The thought cheered her and she set the alarm. Instead of her sunrise yoga class, she would walk to the market.

It was not yet dawn when she left the temple compound of her guesthouse and made her way along the path in the semi-dark, past the rice paddies, to the stairs that descended into the town. An old man walked toward her. She'd seen him before, hunched and carrying bundles of green stalks, but today only a machete swayed from his grip. It was unnerving to encounter anyone wielding such a thing, especially at that hour. Nobody else was around. Not even the woman who sat begging with her two children beneath the tree, its branches creating a creepy canopy over the staircase.

She began her descent, the steps drenched in fog and slick with dew, tangled vines streaming down from above brushed against her face, startling her. She let out a yelp. As a child Drishti had been afraid. Afraid of the dark. Afraid of elevators. Afraid of animals, especially dogs. She also mistrusted dollhouses or anything in miniature. But she liked libraries, oriental rugs, and windows. She was fond of her father's walk-in closet, the orderliness of his suits, the perfect monograms on his shirt cuffs. And she adored his secretary, Miss Pauline, who would sometimes take her to lunch at a deli where they would eat grilled cheese with tomato on rye and sip at chocolate shakes. She had never known her mother.

It had been Stewart's fox terrier Minnie that alleviated her fear of dogs. It had, in fact, been Stewart who had assuaged her fears in general. He was entirely competent in every way. When they'd met, his architecture firm was on the rise and it was not uncommon to see him profiled in magazines. Nearly everyone she introduced him to found a moment to pull her aside and whisper his status as a catch, a hint of envy in their voices, the implication being that they were not quite sure how she'd pulled him to begin with. His only flaw, it seemed, was the fact that he did not want children. She had banked on being able to change his mind, but never managed to. So when he dumped her seven years later for Tad, and the following year they'd given birth to Stewart's daughter by surrogate, those same whisperers turned smug, even sneered.

The fact that it never occurred to her to hold her ground or to do what everyone later told her she should have done—finagle the apartment out of the deal—had been both her undoing and her salvation. She became a nomad in her own city, living in one Airbnb after another, month after month, neighborhood after neighborhood, unable to sign a lease or commit to anything other than the week ahead. All of that had eventually brought her here. To this country. This island. This village.

But first there had been the extended panic. The fears that Stewart had helped her conquer had not actually disappeared, as if he'd been tending them all along in her absence, finally wrapping them up in a precarious package to be returned to her when she moved out of the home they'd shared. She took her fear—it seemed to be the only thing she could actually lay claim to—and she left everything else, all the finds from their weekends spent at flea markets, estate sales, or in dusty shops. She left all of the curated collections that she and Stewart had loved—vintage Italian espresso pots, oil paintings with dogs, midcentury modern lamps, Kurdish tapestries. The Fornasetti plates he had found for her at the flea market in Arezzo, the time he'd taken a business trip to Italy without her. So many things.

Still, it was also liberating. Living without any objects. Seeing what passed for interior design in other people's homes: the anonymity of the furniture, artwork, and items cluttering the apartments she rented had offered a kind of relief. But the disorder also bothered her. It began with the closets. But then, what hadn't, she thought. First she reorganized the bathroom and bedroom storage of a prewar walk-up on West 4th. The spaces were small and demanded order. Next she revamped the kitchen cabinets and the linen closet in a doorman building near Gramercy.

It had actually been Tad who suggested the business idea. She had been seated beside him at the crowded counter of Cafe Gitane while staying on Prince and Elizabeth in what seemed to be an illegal, but adorable, rooftop studio with a to-die-for terrace and a black cat named Toonces who hid under the bed, but came with the rental. Tad's stool had only been occupied by a leather jacket and a cashmere scarf when she arrived. He turned up soon enough, having stepped outside to take a call. Probably from Stewart. At that point she had already ordered, and it was too late to ditch, but rather than cry into her Salade Niçoise she'd made a joke about her new job as an unpaid closet organizer.

"You've always had a knack for interiors."

She appreciated his making the best of an uncomfortable situation. She liked Tad, had clicked with him immediately. She just never imagined that dragging Stewart to the atelier where he designed fabric would have ended as it had. All she'd wanted were window treatments.

"You should hang up a shingle." He waved down his check. "Maybe even trade your services and stay for free."

And there it was, the sense of order she had craved became her profession.

The next day, she gave notice at the tony gallery where she'd long worked.

Her boss, Myles, had seemed flabbergasted. "Have you been smoking crack?" Then relieved. "Well at least I won't have to see you waifing about with those dark circles under your eyes anymore."

A year later, she was the one being profiled, for a story about the top five closet organizers in the city. The journalist had wanted to run a photograph of her in her own closet, and even though she reveled in her newfound expertise, she vowed only to deal with other people's clutter, and had kept on living in temporary housing, streamlining her wardrobe even further, and continuing along the path of no possessions. She'd responded that she had no closet, apartment, or office to photograph, which somehow made the journalist even happier. The piece received so many clicks that her client list grew ten-fold, keeping her busy. But not enough to blot out the birth of Stewart and Tad's daughter Celeste or the terror of bumping into them while they pushed their jogging stroller along the High Line on a Sunday morning.

Drishti pressed on, determined not to be afraid. She made her way down to the main road, turning toward town. It was daybreak when she passed the museum she had never visited. She gazed up at the artist's former home perched at the top of a long ribbon of road and wondered what it contained. Another day, she thought, crossing the road and making her way onto the high bridge over the gorge. It was the only time she had been on the bridge when there was no traffic, and she could hear the rush of the river beneath her. She watched the first rays of sun alight on Pura Gunung Lebah below, standing for a long time looking out over the dark structure of the temple with its deities and towers rising up toward the Campuan Ridge.

Before long, everything began to hum at a higher octave, scooters and taxis passed by, the town beginning to wake. She continued on her way. A few people arrived alongside her on what could not really be called a sidewalk. One of Drishti's greatest fears during her time in Asia had not been traveling alone—that went without saying—but falling into an open sewer. Or really any one of the massive holes that seemed to populate the broken pavement she continually traversed. As a result, she often missed what there might have been to see, so concerned was she with the pitfall of potential injury, even being swallowed entirely. Still worse was her fear nobody would note her absence. And yet, as she walked along the road into town she felt the semblance of a newfound synergy. Maybe just the promise of it. She vowed to hike the Campuan Ridge before she left.

But first the market, she thought.

Although the idea of embracing anything culinary beyond boiling water for tea was out, she filled her canvas bag with small orange globes called maracujá and a few spikey dragon fruit, eschewing the bananas and the despised durian. Her first transaction emboldened her and she set her sights on ginger and lemongrass, picking her way through the produce, past the different sellers, some with elaborate, colorful stacks of fruit, others with their goods laid out on tarps, or in plastic buckets which she steered clear of, for fear of a reprise. She hoped to avoid anything as yet living or even freshly dead.

Glancing around, she recognized him, even from a distance. He was easily six inches taller than most of the Balinese and, in this case, he was actually a foot taller than the woman selling ginger, tamarind, and chili peppers.

Kenneth Love Billings.

His business card had somehow gone missing.

But now here he was.

"I knew you would find me when the time was right," Kenneth Love Billings said.

And when she didn't answer, "What are you planning to do with all the passion fruit?"

"Passion fruit?"

"Those," he pointed at the bag she'd set down on the ground beside her.

"These are maracujá."

"Maracujá. Markisa. Passion fruit," he said. "Same difference."

She'd been eating the maracujá for weeks not knowing what they were. Yet another instance of her disconnection from the natural world. It seemed she'd only recognize the fruit if it were served up to her in the form of a Moscow Mule on girls' night out. Not that she could even recall such a thing. While Kenneth Love Billings paid for his purchases, Drishti picked up her tote, deciding to skip the ginger and repair to the nearest café. She did not say goodbye, but waved vaguely in his direction.

"The name comes from missionaries," Kenneth Love Billings said. He had caught up to her as she crossed the street and followed her into a café.

"Name?"

"The Passion of Christ," he said. "Passion fruit."

His tone was solemn, but his Howdy Doody looks were at odds with his chosen profession. Or calling. Whatever it was. She wanted a cappuccino but had to make due with its vegan cousin, espresso with coconut milk. The barista assured her she'd love it and labored over designing an intricate heart in the foam just to prove it. Kenneth Love Billings pulled a thermos from his pack and filled it with filtered water from the communal pitcher. He told her he did not take caffeine.

While Drishti stirred and sipped, he lobbied for her to attend a consultation session the next evening. He had the air of someone at an AA meeting in a windowless basement. She'd twice stayed in an Airbnb across from the Perry Street Workshop and had watched the comings and goings of its attendees with great curiosity, contemplating how many missed 12-Step meetings or appointments with sponsors were daily dashed by the siren song of a cocktail at Saint Ambroeus on the corner.

"Sorry," she said. "What?"

"I don't claim to have any special powers," he told her. Soon after, he contradicted himself bragging that more than a few people had called their encounters with him "life changing."

If you can change my life tomorrow night, what's stopping you from changing it now, she wanted to ask, but demurred. They sat in strained silence while she considered the possibility. Surely there could be no harm in a session with Kenneth Love Billings, she reasoned, but she would have preferred an impromptu display of his talents before agreeing to pass by. Some small proof. None was forthcoming.

"Until tomorrow then," he said, excusing himself.

She watched him walk away, having already set her mind against the idea of visiting him the next evening or any other evening at his makeshift office. From the window, she observed the activity of the morning market and the street. Backpackers haggling with taxi drivers, locals whizzing by on scooters, an inordinate number of women of a certain age wearing leggings. Drishti couldn't stop thinking about the so-called Spiritual Advisor. Everyone says you will know your guru when you see him, but she was certain she had not met hers yet.

It was just then she noticed Kenneth Love Billings's backpack beside her things under the table. She picked it up and stepped outside to look for the man, but he'd vanished. She waited nearly an hour at the cafe in hopes that he would return, but he never materialized. The bag was imitation military camouflage and sported a faux-gold charm attached to the zipper pull. Upon closer inspection the trinket seemed to be a pair of hands folded together in prayer. Maybe the Namaste mudra. She deliberated about leaving the backpack at the café, but when she spoke to the barista, he did not recall anyone having been with her, and he preferred not to be responsible for lost articles.

In the end, she hefted it along with her passion fruit back home.

She did not dare open it.

Of course, she wanted to.

She resigned herself to bringing it to Billings the following night, but the idea of it somehow threw her off her game, a ridiculous expression implying that, at some point, she'd actually had game. Still, each time she noticed his pack on the chair, she felt a nervousness pulse through her. A restlessness she could not place. She thought about Stewart. She reminded herself not to think about Stewart. She thought about what she would do when she went home. She wondered if it would matter if she never returned home at all. She reminded herself not to think about that either. She tried to meditate, but could not sit still or get comfortable.

In the late afternoon, she attended a yoga class but never fully dropped into it. The teacher was not the one she'd expected. Actually, it was the first time she had ever practiced with a male instructor. The studio was bliss—perched on a high ridge with windows all around, a view of volcanoes in the distance—but all that yang energy had distracted her.

Afterward, she sat in her favorite café hoping to write in her journal. Nothing worked.

Drishti had lost her drishti.

Apart from the Pregnant Swede, the crew from the visa-run were all in attendance: Man Bun, the Aussie, the Reflexologist with the shaved head, even the Standoffish Writer. They weren't exactly paying homage to Kenneth Love Billings—most weren't even queuing up. That said, the café was already jammed. It seemed unlikely any of them might get a shot at a consultation. The backpack weighed heavily on both Drishti's mind and shoulder, but she observed that now was not the moment to hand it off to its owner, for Kenneth Love Billings appeared to be in some sort of trance. And who was sitting across from him but Goddess Girl.

The two sat in facing chairs, hands joined, eyes closed.

Gone were the Spiritual Advisor's dungarees, replaced by a brocade sarong and even a black and white udeng wrapped about his head. Gone, too, was the temporary goddess tattoo that spiraled the length of the girl's leg when she'd climbed into the van for Denpasar. Only a sparkly smudge now evident near her ankle. Other customers were standing, sitting, leaning wherever they could, all staring at Kenneth Love Billings, rapt, even though nothing at all seemed to be happening.

"Ever notice how hard it is to get a cocktail in this town?"

The no-longer-Standoffish Writer pulled out a rattan chair and gestured for Drishti to join her. She sat down, relieved, slinging the backpack, which seemed to have grown heavier by the minute, onto the ground beside her. The menu came sliding across the table for Drishti to examine.

"I'd kill for something a bit stronger than a smoothie."

She was right. Not a drop of alcohol. But there were three types of Kombucha on offer, plus an entire page of tonics and elixirs and power drinks in a variety of configurations. Confronted with so many options, her usual ginger-lime-honey was relegated to the banal.

"I guess I'll go for the Super Nova," Drishti said, "though I hadn't actually planned to stick around."

"Oh, wait for the spectacle, won't you?" The Writer nodded toward Kenneth Love Billings who was now sliding his fingers into Goddess Girl's ears. Drishti had imagined him going the route of the charismatic or speaking in tongues, but she hadn't supposed he would try to pass himself off as a Balian healer.

The waiter took their drink order. The cafe grew more crowded. Goddess Girl had tears rolling down her cheeks. The Spiritual Advisor got up and walked around behind her and held his large palms near her kidneys reiki style, not quite touching them. Drishti looked back to the Writer. She was of indeterminate age. She might have been thirty-five. She might have been fifty. She mentioned that she, too, was from New York, although she'd been living in Europe for "too many years to count." First in Prague. Then Berlin. But she could never cope with the way the city got dark at three in the afternoon. She'd defected to Athens to take advantage of the climate and the fall in rent prices after the Euro crisis.

"I came here to do a magazine piece about tourism decimating the island," she said.

"It does seem the most discovered place on earth," Drishti concurred.

"That was two years ago."

It was not difficult to see how this might happen. After all, even Drishti had stayed longer than planned, which was how the two had met, although they had never properly introduced themselves as such.

To that end, Drishti had not yet announced herself as Drishti to anyone and the prospect of using her new name made her bashful. When the drinks arrived, they both tested their concoctions with bamboo straws. More passion fruit.

It's all about the passion whenever Kenneth Love Billings is around, she noted.

And yet it actually wasn't.

The Writer explained how she'd been renewing her tourist visa again and again by flying to Singapore for passport stamps, only going the way of fingerprinting and immigration for this last round. She'd come to the café because she'd been toying with an essay about the ongoing relevance of the quest. And Drishti filled her in on how she'd accidentally acquired Billings's backpack, making sure it was clear she had not come seeking spiritual advice.

The Writer leaned forward, sweeping a lock of auburn hair from her eyes, "You took it home and you never opened it?"

Drishti shook her head.

"Impressive." But her tone indicated otherwise, as if it were a failing, at the very least an inexcusable lack of curiosity.

"Every time I went near it I got a strange vibe." It was true, Drishti thought. Even seeing it on her chair had been a distraction. "I just couldn't."

"Are you always so restrained?"

"Yes."

Then, "No."

Then, "I don't know. Sometimes."

"Let's just take a peek."

It was really all Drishti needed. Permission. A coconspirator.

The Writer excused herself a moment, requesting that Drishti please wait before making a move on the backpack. Goddess Girl stood up and hugged Kenneth Love Billings. She looked transformed. But she did not look rejuvenated. It wasn't that she'd aged exactly, but something was different. Not necessarily in a good way from what Drishti could see. But that was not the way Goddess Girl played it. She flipped her blond dreads over her shoulder, her movements exaggerated as if she were drunk.

"I know you prefer dollars," she said.

She pulled a wad of rupiah out of a tooled leather holster-like belt that was slung over her narrow hips and kitted out with a change-purse and a pocket for a smartphone, explaining to whomever was paying attention that it was the only currency she had, but for a few Ringgit left from "a stopover in KL."

She hugged the Spiritual Advisor again.

By the time she let go of him, the Aussie had usurped her chair and sat gazing up at the tall man before her. There were a dozen others who seemed to be waiting, whether or not they were in a designated order was debatable. Beyond that, there were many more curious observers surging into available pockets of space. Drishti wondered if the café gave Billings a cut on drink sales, mocktails or otherwise. She vacillated between hoping that they did and preferring they didn't.

When the Writer returned, refreshed, which is to say wearing lipstick, Drishti discovered the backpack was no longer next to her chair.

Nothing gets stolen in Bali.

Or that was what everyone said.

They scanned the bar, searched under nearby tables, and asked around, but agreed their collective effort was to no avail.

"It'll turn up," the Writer said. "Just not here, not tonight. You'll see."

Drishti couldn't decide if it would be worth telling Kenneth Love Billings she had rescued his backpack from one café only to have it be stolen at another while in her care. She glanced over at him. He was deep into his session with the Aussie. The two sat in facing chairs, the would-be guru leaning forward and gesturing with both hands, as if fashioning a mudra. His voice was too low to hear over the general din. The woman's eyelids fluttered. Otherwise she wore no expression.

The Writer checked her WhatsApp and announced she was ready to bail. They walked together to the cashier. Drishti picked up the tab for the Super Nova and her companion's Milky Way. She took one last look around. Goddess Girl was in heated conference with a woman who could be her twin. And there sat Man Bun, perched on a barstool with Kenneth Love Billings in his sights, too engrossed to notice anyone else.

Outside, there seemed to be a deficit of taxis and Drishti couldn't find Putu the Driver's card, or any of the other cards that had been pressed into her palm over the last few weeks. She had accumulated plenty, all conveniently gathered in a bowl on her kitchen counter. The Writer said she would offer her a lift, but she hadn't thought to bring a spare helmet. Drishti thanked her anyway, relieved to have an excuse not to join her. She was terrified of scooters.

"Such a pity you never even got a peek at that pack," the Writer said. She lowered the windscreen on her helmet and drove away.

Alone, Drishti despaired at the thought of walking back in the dark. The location had been much further away than she'd expected. It sat isolated on a long curving stretch of road in the middle of nowhere. She resolved to ask one of the employees to call her a taxi. Peering in from the doorway, she considered giving it one last look, just in case the backpack had been rifled through and abandoned but was still, in some sense, intact. But she worried any reconnaissance would only further entangle her in the Kenneth Love Billings show. At that moment, the Aussie came barreling outside, bumping into Drishti.

The Reflexologist soon trailed after.

"What happened?" Drishti asked.

"He's got a gift," the Aussie cried, collapsing into the Reflexologist's arms and howling. It was unclear what emotion her tears implied, but before long the Reflexologist had calmed her—without touching the woman's feet—and the Aussie's wails softened into hiccups.

Meanwhile, Man Bun arrived on the scene.

"Dude," he said. "You should've seen it."

But when she asked what exactly she had missed he offered up nothing of note, wishing them all a "Namaste" before kick-starting his scooter and zooming off.

At this point, Drishti decided to come clean with the Spiritual Advisor about the missing backpack, and walked back into the crowded cafe. There, Kenneth Love Billings stood in his sarong, towering over his acolytes, arms open wide, palms facing heavenward, eyes closed. A moment later, he blinked several times as if the dim lights were painful to him. He shushed the seekers, announcing that he needed to take a break, the sessions physically drained him if he did too many in a row. His groupies scattered, welcoming his words as a cue to check their iPhones or order another elixir. Drishti alone stood beside the man's table.

When he saw her, he stood up, drew his thin lips into a smile and reached out, placing a hand on either of her shoulders in an awkward greeting made still more awkward by the fact that he continued to rest his rough, sweaty palms on her bare skin while she spoke.

She attempted to unravel the story of the backpack, but as she did so Kenneth Love Billings grew more and more agitated.

"And then it was just—gone," she said.

He stared at her with pale eyes, his smile transforming into what could only be described as a snarl, and he pulled her closer, to whisper in her ear. She could feel his sour breath on her neck, his razor stubble grazing her cheek. She sprung back from his touch, knocking over a chair and falling.

Above her, his tall figure was black in the lamplight, casting a shadow over her.

"You have failed a great test," Kenneth Love Billings said in a voice loud enough for everyone to hear.

Drishti climbed to her feet, stifled a sob, and brushed past him, fleeing the cafe. Without hesitation, she set off on foot along the crumbling shoulder of the impossibly dark road. Something that, twenty minutes earlier, she wouldn't have considered doing. Intermittently, cars and scooters passed, casting beams of light through the fog and illuminating the tall trees in flashes. Invisible roosters crowed, and the distant clanging of gamelan echoed an eerie soundtrack in the darkness. She had no idea which direction the temple lay or what ritual they were celebrating. She looked up at the moon. Only the edge of it glowed from behind a cloud. It was at times like these that she wondered exactly what she had been expecting when she'd come to this small island. Why anyone expects anything at all from traveling. She recalled what the Writer had told her about the ongoing inevitability of the quest.

She hadn't realized she was on one until now.

The stop in Padang Bai was not a bus stop at all but an open-air warung facing out onto a busy street. There were three scratched metal tables with rickety chairs resting on the grimy cement floor. An elderly man wearing a sarong and no shirt sat on a low stool reading the Jakarta Post. The women who worked in the kitchen—essentially a counter with a cutting board, two burners, and a wok—chatted back and forth, laughing. Drishti loved the sound of the language but had only been able to replicate the most rudimentary phrases. She wondered if it would ever seep in, if she'd ever get over her shyness to speak it. While she waited for the minivan to take her to the stop near Pura Goa Lawah, she watched a fair-haired woman with an extreme tan drive up and park. She took off her helmet and hung it from the handlebars. Speaking Indonesian, she ordered nasi campur and ate every bite from what could only be described as a filthy plate. Drishti could not imagine a scenario in which she would ever truly go native as this woman had, yet she felt no desire to leave the island.

She was just about to get up the courage to use the bathroom when she saw a rat trot from beneath a parked car into the warung, headed for the kitchen. After the dead rat episode, live ones were somehow preferable. Anyway, she was becoming somewhat accustomed to such things. A smallish rat hung about near the Ganesha statue that sat sentinel beside the steps leading up to her apartment. As with the gecko, she preferred to believe it was a single rat living close to her front door. And as with the myth, this rat was simply Ganesha's attendant, rather than a rodent carrying disease. She had spotted the deity's sidekick scampering among the flowers near the breakfast table as she ate her usual pineapple pancake and tried to connect to the interminably slow Wi-Fi. Eventually, she'd given up on the Internet altogether upon discovering her required software update would take six days to load. It was then she'd had to admit how many hours she'd squandered at that table trying to make contact with her old life, even if it meant hanging out in proximity to a rat.

When she'd pointed the rodent out to Nyoman, the woman had laughed and said, "Oh, the mouse?"

She decided Nyoman was actually rather genius, her limited vocabulary in English making her something of a sage. Drishti adored their conversations. She loved the whole family, the son who spoke of visions and magic without irony, telling her in spite of his desire to be an engineer he was constrained by birth to be a Balian medicine man, the little brother in his neatly pressed school clothes, the beautiful daughter Kadek who was the go-between for Nyoman and her husband with all the guests. It had been Kadek who recommended Pura Goa Lawah.

Drishti hadn't expected the transit to be so protracted. She'd set out hours ago, but there had been a glitch with one of the vans breaking down. And here she sat in the heat, sticking to her metal chair, too afraid to drink or eat anything but for the bottle of water she'd broken the seal on when the first minivan dropped her off. She'd been half betting, half hoping the next driver would be named Putu. It was something like six for six now, but no, when the van pulled up and the young guy behind the wheel clambered out, he said he was called Wayan. Still, he was the first-born, she thought, in keeping with the

Balinese naming custom, like all the Putu's who'd driven her along the way. It almost counted.

A couple in matching Birkenstocks tumbled out of the van, asking after the bathroom. Drishti wanted to warn them about the filth, about the whole situation, really, but they whizzed by. The girl came back first. Then the guy. They spoke Italian and seemed alarmed about something, gesturing like crazy. She assumed they'd met the rat.

"Do either of you want the front?" Drishti asked.

"No tanks," the guy said. He had a lovely smile. They both did.

Along the way, they chatted a bit, even though it was a challenge for Drishti to look back at the couple without getting motion sickness. They were Sardinian. She was Marta and he was Flavio. They were on their way up the coast to Amed.

"To free dive," Marta said.

"There is a sheep," Flavio added. "Under the water."

"A sheep?"

"Sì—the peoples all say it is very beautiful to swim inside the sheep."

Marta nodded and smiled in agreement.

Drishti was stumped. She tried another tack. "What makes it free?"

They looked at each other, discussing their response at length in Italian.

"No tanks," Flavio finally said.

It was a mile or so up the road before Drishti stopped imagining an enormous sheep waterlogged and resting at the bottom of the sea and tweaked that the Italians would be diving the wreck. She'd read about a naval ship off the coast of Tulamben, then forgotten about it. She pictured it marooned there, alone in the dark, and felt something surge up in her like the rush of air when a door unexpectedly blows open. Everything went on as before but she no longer heard it: the driver's incessant phone calls, the chatter in the van, the unexpected stopping at a rudimentary petrol station, and the other passengers getting in and out, the shuffling of seats—all of it fell away replaced by an absolute craving the likes of which she'd never known, a longing to dive in. She imagined herself there. The dark sand sparkling, the pitch-black water, and the volcano in the distance. She knew now that she must go.

As Wayan pulled into the bus stop at Candi Dasa, she felt far more than a flicker of longing to continue on with the Italians all the way up to Amed. But she had only prepared for one day out. She decided to keep on with her plan. There will be time for Amed, she thought, having bought herself another month's stay with the visa run. Her original flight back to JFK had already departed without her. It was something she'd never done in her life—simply not turning up for a non-refundable ticket. And she had yet to book a new one.

She gathered up her things, said goodbye to the Italians, and double-checked with Wayan about the pick-up time. He reminded her that it would be the last shuttle and not to miss it. She stepped down from the vehicle, and Marta and Flavio called out the window.

"We are waiting for you in Amed," Marta said.

"Sì, you must to come dive the sheep," Flavio added.

Drishti waved at them and watched the minivan pull away.

She got into the first car in the line, asking the young man to take her to Pura Goa Lawah. The driver offered to stick around and bring her back. She wasn't sure how much time she would need, but she didn't want to feel rushed. She asked when the temple closed and he said, "Hindu Gods always working." She took this to mean the temple never shut. They agreed on a time in the early evening. He handed her his card, inscribed with the image of Ganesha and his faithful mouse, his contact info just below. His name was Putu.

She had brought no guidebook along, not just today, but for the entire journey. She'd been determined to let things unfold as they might. It meant for more complicated negotiations in new places, but that had been part of the pact she'd made with herself when she set off from New York. So far it had worked, slowly beginning to liberate her from a long-held difficulty making up her mind. From the fear of making mistakes: she had made plenty.

Foreigners had to purchase tickets and Drishti was the only one in line. She'd been advised to wear a sarong and the man nodded at her in approval as she paid him. She followed two local women dressed in the traditional lace kebaya, each balancing a large woven basket on her head. Two large banyan trees flanked the entrance to the compound. There were no doors, just a forlorn pair of facing gates that looked like dark wings on either side as she crossed over the threshold.

She hadn't realized the temple would be so close to the shoreline with its black sand beach. Nusa Penida seemed to float in the distance on the dark expanse of water. As a child she had once traveled to Santa Lucia with her father and that was her only memory of such a beach. There had been a riptide their first day on the island and it had pulled her out to sea. After the incident, she had never once risked swimming in the ocean. She recalled now, the feeling of being immersed in those cobalt waters, to swim and swim and swim finding herself still further from shore. Her father's voice calling out to her and the way it grew softer with each stroke. The endless expanse of blue and the desire to give in to the undertow completely.

She tried to shake off the image, giving her attention to the temple complex. Inside, there were more banyans with twisted roots, their wide branches providing umbrellas of shade. Stone sculptures swathed in black, white, and gold fabric greeted her, each adorned with colorful flowers and extravagant stacks of fruit and pastries, one even had a row of Coke Zero cans, in case the gods were watching their waistlines, she mused. Thin twines of smoke drifted up from incense tucked into the offerings, she watched it rise noticing a golden bat high up among the embellishments decorating one of the altars. She continued on, past the Meru towers with their funky thatched roofs, leaving the temple, and moved toward the sea with an urgency she had only just begun to feel.

She dug through her bag for her hat, pulling it low to shade her face, and sat on the beach staring out across the Badung Strait toward the island. There were no other people nearby. The sea was black and calm, save one long white line of surf breaking along the shore. A ferryboat made its way toward the island. She ran her fingers through the warm sand, unable to take her eyes from the water yet conscious of the temple and its ominous cave looming at her back.

Earlier that morning, the first cool breeze in memory had blown through her veranda, fluttering the coconut palms and playing a soft melody on the bamboo chimes hanging there. Drishti slid open the glass door and found her sandals where she'd left them. The three scruffy dogs that slept outside her door were already waiting for her, stretching or dancing in place. The dogs had trailed her for the last leg of her journey the night of the debacle with Kenneth Love Billings. At first, she'd been afraid. Three pairs of glowing eyes rushed out of the dark when she turned onto the dirt path leading home. They continued on behind her, past the rice paddies all the way to her door, at which point she decided she was grateful for the escort, offering them a bowl of water. It seemed any small tenderness was enough. For nearly a week, the dogs returned each night to sleep on her doorstep, often following her in the mornings to yoga or the café. One black, one white, one gold—the same colors adorning the deities in the temples.

She and the dogs padded down the steps, past Ganesha to the path, where she put her sandals on. All around the garden began to wake in a jumble of color. Dew on everything. There were more shades of green than she knew names for. And so many flowers. From the flame red of the hibiscus to the pink blossoms of the frangipani, and the yellow and white clusters of the moringa. And still others. She walked along, relishing every blossom, every color. It wasn't that she was seeing the flowers for the first time, but that it was the first time she could actually see them. At the back of the compound was a small pavilion dedicated to Saraswati, goddess of knowledge, and there a lotus had sprung up amidst the water lilies, its purple petals just beginning to open.

Even though Nyoman and the others would soon be making their daily offerings, she decided to gather some flowers for the Ganesha who guarded her door. She could hear the splash of the koi jumping in the little pond as she plucked several hibiscus flowers. The dogs shadowed her as she carried the blooms back to her apartment and arranged them in a small glass. She had learned that Ganesha loved the color red and so that is what she brought for him. He also liked treats, so she plucked a mango out of the nearest tree for good measure. She wasn't clear if she needed him to remove an obstacle or to put one in her way—so unsure was she about the path she now found herself on—but either way, she felt it couldn't hurt to enlist his help before she set off that morning.

Drishti walked further along Kusamba beach where she found a hut with a thatched roof selling small parcels of the local sea salt along with coconuts and other drinks. She spent a long time in the shade sipping at her coconut and staring out at the dark sea. Nearby, a woman sat on the ground making offerings, each one an intricate collage of purple bougainvillea, white and yellow jasmine, a cookie, and a stick of incense inside a small container made from palm leaves. Drishti smiled and the woman offered to teach her. Surrounded by the sweet scent of flowers and lulled by the sound of the surf, it was a calming occupation.

She realized, however, that she'd been avoiding the main event and admonished herself for not having chosen the temple with all the fountains for her first foray. She fairly quaked at the idea of the cave, said to contain healing waters and a path that led some thirty kilometers through the mountain to the sacred Mother Temple at the foot of the volcano. The Balinese freely admitted nobody had explored the cavern for centuries. Legend held that Goa Lawah was home to an enormous snake—or naga—that wore a golden crown and feasted upon the thousands of bats living inside the cave. Even if the snake was a myth, the bats were real. What could she possibly have been thinking? And why did she feel so compelled to witness it? She could barely cope with one small bat flying in her window. How would she ever have the composure to visit the cave? She thanked the woman who insisted on giving Drishti an offering to bring to Goa Lawah.

It was nearly dusk when she arrived back at the temple, armed with an offering of her own making. She felt inspired to participate in some aspect of the ceremony. She would begin at a moderate distance and work her way up to it, she thought, feeling consoled by the fact that Putu would soon arrive to retrieve her. She made her way past the outer pavilions and as she approached the cave, she could see several small altars adorning its entrance. Overhead, thick vines covered the steep hillside and dangled down, framing the mouth of the cave. Off to the side, a group of Balinese men and women prayed, and an assortment of tourists and locals gathered, looking expectantly at the shrine.

She could smell the bats before she could see them. Or rather, she could smell the bat shit from several meters away. She alone climbed the few steps leading up to the cave. She clutched the offering and forced herself to take small steps forward to place it on the altar. She'd lost the stick of incense somewhere along the way. The woman had told her the bougainvillea was for protection, so she was relieved to see the purple petals and even the cookie were intact. She balanced her offering atop a tall stack layered with many others. Obviously she was not Balinese, nor was she suddenly converting to Hinduism, yet the gesture made her feel connected somehow. Whether to something dormant or something nascent, she could not say, but the ritual gave her the courage to move beyond the altar. Sacred site or not, she still had to contend with the bats.

They'll be sleeping, she told herself.

Only they weren't.

She could hear a great rustling. What had first appeared to be dark volcanic stone or even mud making up the walls and ceiling of the cave, she now saw was undulating and entirely alive, covered with black bats. Bats upon bats upon bats. Hanging above her. Wedged in beside one another and clinging to the walls on either side of her, filling the cave for as far as she could see.

You're here now, she thought. Just step inside.

She inched ahead, bit by bit, till she dared not go further.

It wasn't that the bats screeched so much as chirped, but the chirping was greatly amplified inside the cave, their strange song echoing over her.

First, a single bat unfolded its intricate wings and dropped from the ceiling, swooping past her on its way out of the cave. Then another and another and another. She stood, too petrified to even close her eyes: she was directly in their flight path. Before she could even think to cover her head or bolt away, more bats flew straight at her, flapping and fluttering toward her by the hundreds, surrounding her with their webbed wings and only funneling about her at the very last second.

Although she did not recall evacuating the cave or climbing down the steps, she found herself outside, facing a small group of people. To the onlookers who'd gathered to watch the evening exodus, it must have appeared as if a woman had dropped from the sky, deposited before them by the colony of bats. Everyone stood gawking at the phenomenon—both at Drishti and at the chaotic cloud of bats rising from the cave to darken the dark blue above.

"Dude, you are one serious badass," she heard someone say. "Props."

She turned away from the small crowd to face the sky, watching until all the bats had finally exited the cave and taken flight.

There was traffic along the two-lane road back to Candi Dasa. Putu slowed to nearly a crawl, eventually stopping altogether behind several cars. A couple on a Vespa sputtered up beside them. The driver tried to maneuver through the narrow space between cars, but was forced to stop. From the backseat, Drishti could see their silver helmets, the windscreens covering their faces. They were so close to her window she could have reached out and touched them. The driver's bare arms revealed the feathered edge of a large tattoo. The girl straddling him wore a camouflage backpack. The traffic eased up and the Vespa shot ahead. In the glare of Putu's headlights, she caught a glimpse of the girl's blonde dreadlocks swaying side to side and the glimmer of something metallic, before they disappeared.

When Putu pulled the car over in Candi Dasa, idling in front of the shuttle stop, nobody was there and it was clear she had missed the van. This, she understood, had been inevitable. Whenever anybody warns you not to be late for the last bus, you are always sure to miss it.

"Shall I find someone to drive you back to Ubud, Miss?"

"Can't you bring me?"

He apologized, explaining it was too far out of his way. He shared the taxi with his brother and had to return the car to him. Their sister owned a guesthouse, and his brother was scheduled to pick up guests arriving very late at the airport. She asked where his family lived and he told her Amed.

"Then take me to Amed, instead."

"You are sure?"

"Yes," she said. "It's perfect."

She might see the Italians, after all, she thought. Maybe even the sheep. She sent a message to Nyoman not to worry, she'd be back in a few days, and asked her to please give the dogs some water.

"You have sisters and brothers, Miss?" Putu asked.

"No," she said. "There's only me."

"Then your name also Putu," he said, rechristening her, yet again.

He turned the car around and they set out, heading back in the direction of the temple, the night air rushing in through the open windows.

Drishti felt light—as if the wings of all those bats sweeping over her had somehow managed to unburden her of whatever it was she'd been carrying. She looked out toward the beach and the smooth dark surface of the Bali Sea. The last bend of light glittering violet along the horizon where it met the night sky, now almost entirely black. The Pura Goa Lawah bats were no longer visible, but she knew they were still out there. Somewhere. High overhead. Swirling and swooping in a tumultuous cloud.

eightball

I stare at him, barefooted, a thread-worn prayer rug beneath his bony, veiny feet. Still tan from last summer. I remember the rug from his bedroom. It was antique even then, but today in the striated sunlight through his blinds it appears ragged. The bright red and turquoise geometry faded to soft coral swirls, the threadbare melancholy of no longer blue. He leans from the sofa over the low coffee table. Slow ballet. Razorblade in hand, cutting lines on a framed black and white photograph, an early one of mine. The beach. Our beach. Those grassy dunes that poked us, the soft white sand that soothed us, the cold gray sea we loved so well.

I can't look at it.

So I look at him.

At his tanned feet beneath us.

At the way our hands are the same.

My brother wears a gold band on his ring finger. The ring was made from a pair of Papa's cufflinks, an initial for each wrist. The band is beveled and wraps around squaring at the top into the letter P. On my own hand is the mate, the Q, but I wear it on my index finger, because it's too big. I can't wear it on my right hand because it catches when I'm advancing film or adjusting the shutter. Only now does it occur to me that neither of us is named after anyone in my father's family. The cufflink-rings, like the oriental carpet, were passed down from our mother's side. In a way, even the beach we inherited from her.

In the distance I see Patrick and my mother on the path through the dunes. They each have a handle of a picnic basket they lug between them. My mother could probably carry it herself but this is our ritual. My father and I start the fire while she and Patrick gather everything else in the kitchen and load up the basket. If we're fast enough we can even get the bacon into the skillet before they arrive.

My father kneels beside the small fire and places the grill on top of the flames with a pair of tongs. He's got a blanket spread out, weighted with a heavy cast iron skillet, a carton of eggs, some bacon, a spatula, and a thermos full of coffee. When he lifts the skillet, I have to sit on the blanket so the corners don't whip around in the wind and dust everything with sand.

I'm shivering in my shorts and swimsuit.

"Want my sweater?"

I nod and he pulls it off and tosses it to me and I wrap it round me like a cape. My father's sweater smells like summer, like smoke and suntan lotion, sun-dried cotton and saltwater. I unscrew the red plastic lid from the thermos, fill it with coffee, and attempt a big sip. It's steaming and bitter and I immediately spit it out in the sand. He teases me, taking the cup back and standing, legs spread wide, staring down at the fire.

"I think she's ready," he says. "Scalpel?" I hand him the spatula.

My mother and Patrick put the basket down on the blanket and Patrick takes off toward the water, yelling back at me over his shoulder. I jump up, the sweater falling behind me as I chase after him. The two of us splash around in the shallow water and look for shells. Early morning is the best time to find them.

"Look at this one," Patrick says. "Or this one?"

His hands are full and we examine each one carefully, some bleached white and smooth, others flamed with stripes, gold and orange. Patrick lines the best ones up, side by side, where the sand is sure to stay dry. I take the rest and throw them back into the surf. When we get bored with our search, we grab a couple of sticks and poke at a jellyfish that's washed up with the tide. A big wave rolls in. We run and scream then chase it back out where it came from.

Dizzy comes lumbering toward us. Her coat is soaked and she's carrying the remains of a crab in her mouth. She drops it at our feet and begins to shake. She always waits till she's right up on you to shake.

"You're stinky, Diz!"

"Like fish," Patrick says.

She lies down and rolls around in the sand, kicking her legs in the air. Dizzy's part golden retriever, part nobody knows for sure. Her ears stick up like a shepherd's, only they're huge. Dizzy's been around longer than me. My father gave her as a present to our mother when Patrick was still small.

"Dizzy Gespy," I say, stroking her ears.

"Gillespie," Patrick tells me.

"Who's that?"

"Some jazz guy."

"But Dizzy's a girl."

"Doesn't matter."

The beach is ours alone. The sun gleams violet on the water as it breaks through low clouds and rises over the sea.

"Breakfast!"

We rush over to the blanket, now set like a table, plates and silverware, a bowl full of blueberries. I plop down beside my mother. She's wearing one of my father's white button-downs over her bikini. Cuffs rolled up and her gold charm bracelet loose on her wrist. Her legs are long and smooth, loaded with freckles. She always seems glamorous to me, even at the beach. Her hair, red like mine but past her chin, has a paisley scarf tied in it. My father is dark, broad-shouldered and strong. His swim trunks look like canvas, only shiny, with white laces that tie up the front. When he smiles his eyes crinkle up, almost closed.

"I was a lifeguard on this beach." He stares out at the sea. "During college."

"You were?" Of course I already know this. Everybody does.

He worked at the beach club, crisp white umbrellas and whitewashed cabanas. Days he sat in the lifeguard chair, zinc oxide covering his nose, a shiny silver whistle clamped between his teeth or dangling from his neck. At night he'd wait tables in the dining room with the rest of the cabana boys. That's where he and my mother met. Her parents were members. Her family has always belonged there. They still do.

My father tells the same story, how he out-swam everyone and saved a couple of kids caught in a riptide so many summers ago.

"Ancient history, Dad," Patrick says. "Let's eat."

Patrick glances up at me. I can barely see the green of his eyes, his pupils so huge the whole iris is black. His face looks tight, almost like he's wincing, even though he's smiling. That smile. Patrick's smile; it was all I ever wanted. Then it's just the top of his head, tilting over the mirror. He's cut his hair short where it is dark at the roots, his childhood curls and blonde long gone.

"Yours."

I lean down to finish what's left.

Bix comes bounding in from the kitchen, nails scratching the parquet. She leaps onto the couch beside Patrick and drops a soggy tennis ball in his lap. Bix is Scotty's neurotic black lab whose only joy is fetching that ball. Patrick rubs the dog's neck and strokes his glossy spine, but Bix only whines and nudges the ball with his nose until Patrick complies, tossing the ball so it ricochets off the baseboard and bounces into the kitchen sending the dog after it.

Dizzy was never really our mother's dog. Nor mine. She always belonged to Patrick. She guarded his stroller, swam with him in the ocean, and accompanied him through all those years until he left for school. By then she'd gone gray, had troublesome hips. I think

Dizzy knew Patrick was gone for good, but she held a vigil in his room, night after night, in case he came home, sleeping on his bed for months.

After getting my license, our parents go out of town, letting me stay alone in the house with Dizzy. One morning I find her, stiff and silent, her muzzle resting on Patrick's pillow. I lie down beside her and cry until my throat aches so that I can feel it up inside my ears. Finally, I stand up and wrap her in Patrick's blanket, lugging her heavy body downstairs, out to the car. I drive for hours, smoking and talking, telling stories to the dead dog that was all I had left of Patrick and our childhood. In the parking lot outside the vet's, I slip her collar over her ears and muzzle, keeping it so I can send the tags to Patrick. I tuck his blanket tight around her and carry her inside.

"You know, Dizzy slept on your bed every night."

I think it was losing Dizzy that made me change my plans and follow him out here. I never intended to head west. But here I am.

"Yeah," he says. "You already told me."

I keep waiting for some conversational crevice to open between us, some path where every lane I choose doesn't end in a cul-de-sac with me going round and round, my brother standing in the center, somehow always with his back to me.

When did we stop talking to one another?

Patrick picks up our empty glasses from the coffee table and carries them into the kitchen. I hear the sound of water running. I look around at his things, trying to figure out what it is our lives are becoming. His pristine living room conveys none of the chaos I expected to find. But it all feels fraught. Tension not so much between us as everywhere around us. The photograph of the beach isn't the only one of mine he's brought from home. Beside the lamp there are two pictures in a small frame that opens like a book. The time we traveled along the coast in Turkey. And just like the rain, it all comes down.

We are in the car when a sudden storm renders the roads nearly impassable, forcing us to wait out the worst of it in a roadside café. More of a shanty really. The sound of rain on the corrugated metal roof. An old woman brings us coffee in small white cups. It's my first time drinking it since that time on the beach with my father. By then, my brother and I had tested much of the liquor in our parents' cabinet, but had never drunk a cup of coffee.

When we finish, the woman offers to read our futures in the grounds, black silt in the bottoms of our cups. After looking into my mother's cup, she places her hands flat on the table and leans forward as if catching her breath. That's when I catch that her left hand is missing two fingers.

"What does it say?" Patrick asks. He looks nervous.

"Nothing." The woman gathers up all the cups and saucers, stacks them into her lame hand. "Not clear."

The night before he had crept out of our room. It was past midnight when I rolled over to see him in the doorway. He whispered not to worry—he'd be back soon. I knew better than to say anything to him. Or to our parents, who'd spent most of the evening drinking and arguing in their adjoining room. I just hoped he wasn't trying to buy anything. Before we'd left, I had overheard Spit joking about Patrick ending up in a Turkish prison and it terrified me. I tried my best to stay awake, but I couldn't. Later still, I woke to the hypnotic din of the call to prayer, found Patrick asleep in his bed, a sliver of moonlight playing over his shoulder.

"It's just superstition, sweetie," our Mom tells him. Her voice is unnaturally cheery as it has been on so much of the trip. She tries to pull Patrick into her embrace but he shrugs off her touch and slouches away, feigns interest in a poster tacked up on the wall. Our mother continues to smile the smile she's mastered. Frosted lipstick. Big dark glasses. How old she seems to me at this moment and yet she is just thirty-five.

Maybe it's all the lines we've done, but each memory is jagged, sharp. The way our father sits with the driver and the other men drinking raki. The sticky pink candies that taste of roses. The tiny white cat leaping into my lap and the sound of her purring. The smell of the sea after the rain. I'd wondered where my photographs from that trip had ended up—probably in some shoebox my mother tossed with the rubbish— so I'm surprised to see my brother still has some of them. Shots of my parents and Patrick amidst sun-bleached Roman ruins. I was enamored with my Polaroid then. The instant gratification of those perfect squares. How you had to hold them carefully along the white border, waving the wet film back and forth. Watching the image rise up out of nothing.

Mandy's house is a little brick bungalow, indistinguishable from all the other little brick bungalows lining the street except for the sagging sofa on the front porch, a cushion missing and the springs poking through. A forsythia bush in yellow flame beside the walkway the only sign of spring. Patrick parks his Triumph in the driveway and we climb off and walk up the stone steps to the porch, peeling off our helmets as we go. We hear music. Patrick knocks and there's a crash from inside followed by several expletives in a booming voice. The door opens just a crack and a brown beard and mouth jut out above the safety chain.

"Get in here," the mouth growls.

The door closes. The door reopens, just wide enough for Patrick and me to pass through. Inside all the shades are drawn and the place reeks of cats and bong water. Cats everywhere. Two sleeping on the huge speakers blaring The Dead. Another darting past as Mandy shuts the door behind us. In the kitchen, there's a scale on the table, a gallon-sized Ziploc nearly a quarter full of coke, more coke on the table, plastic jars of benzocaine or some other anesthetic, razor blades, and a shoebox lid full of small brown glass vials with black screw caps. A few have narrow spoons attached by a hinge. A white film over everything. Paw prints.

Mandy doesn't look like a cokehead. Or even a dealer, really. He's too beefy. His gruff canceled out by a sprinkle of freckles across his nose. He settles into a brown leather office chair, wheels squeaking as he scrapes across the worn linoleum and pulls himself up to the table. His hands are huge, a tattooed bracelet of bones and roses around a puffy right wrist. He nods at a chair and I lift a pile of magazines off the seat and put them on the floor, sit down.

"Always some beautiful woman in tow," Mandy says.

"My little sister," Patrick tells him.

He asks Mandy if he can make a call and wanders off.

"Beer?"

I nod and he leans over to open the fridge. The light is broken. An indecipherable stench wafts out. His massive fist comes back out of the dark with a can of nobody's favorite, Coors. I wipe the top of it with the edge of my shirt. I'm relieved he doesn't offer me a glass—the sink is piled with dirty dishes. Cat hair collects around the edge of the table legs.

I sip the beer and look around, light a cigarette. Mandy makes himself busy spooning coke into the tray on the scale and whistling. He shoos an obese tabby off the table.

"What's your name, Little Sister?"

"Quinn."

"Like the song."

The tabby, or its mutant twin, jumps into my lap and tries to climb onto the table. Mandy gives it a shove. "Get outta here, Jerry." It hisses and leaps onto the counter, navigates through empty pizza boxes toward the window, disappearing behind the curtains.

"Fucking Sonya, fucking cats."

"So, where were we," he gestures toward the table, "eightball?"

"You'll have to ask Trick."

"Trick? Ah, right. But this is actually a treat. Where is that sorry-ass brother of yours?"

Smoke hangs in the air between us.

"Fuck it, let's do a line."

He touches a glass pipe in the ashtray.

"Or would you prefer to base it?"

"Line's fine."

"A line is fine, a line is fine. Would that it were always the time." He laughs. "I think I made a little rhyme."

He scrapes out three fat lines.

I look at the filthy kitchen. What's the point of worrying about germs given the chemicals I'm inhaling. I do the line and hand him back the bill and watch him snuffle up the second line. I swear I can feel it running up from my nasal cavity into my brain. For some reason I only ever snort it up the right side. It can't be good.

Patrick comes back and goes straight to the sink, starts doing dishes.

"Leave that," Mandy says.

"I can't."

He's always been the one who tidied up. He makes quick work of it, arranging all the plates in a little wire rack and clearing the counter of debris. He throws all the take-out containers and such in the trash then opens the freezer in search of vodka and ice to make himself a drink. He joins us at the table, bending over his line.

"Time for a little jazz," Mandy says.

He gets up and goes into the living room to change the album. Crackle of speakers and the song comes on. He ambles back through the doorway.

"You gotta love the Quintet."

Patrick looks at me for an instant then says he has to make another call, pushing himself back from the table and getting up so fast his chair tumbles over.

"Or maybe not," Mandy says. He picks the chair up, unruffled.

Neither of us really listens to jazz anymore.

It only makes us tense.

Or sad.

Both.

My mother marinates the steaks and puts out hors d'oeuvres. My father breaks the seal on a bottle of scotch and pours himself a drink before setting up the bar. He lines everything up, rocks glasses, highballs and a martini shaker next to the bottles, more scotch, some gin, brandy, and sweet vermouth. Patrick fills the silver ice bucket and carries it out to him on the deck.

"Transfusions?" he asks and we nod wildly.

He clinks ice into two tall glasses and pours in grape juice and ginger ale. We drink them down and beg for another then stumble around pretending we're drunk.

When the bar is sufficiently stocked my father goes back inside and puts the speakers in the windowsill. He's always in charge of the music. He and Patrick thumb through his records and choose Miles Davis. The needle falls onto the vinyl with a scratch and a thump. Staccato of horns, then piano, and finally the bass joining in for the first few bars of "So What."

The Madigans ride their bikes over. Libby Madigan's basket brimming with ears of corn purchased that day at the farmers' market. The O'Briens and the Farinellos drive out from town. The Farinellos always show up last, armed with a story about waiting for the raised arms of the bay bridge, the long queue of cars idling as a rickety boat passed beneath. They tumble out of their station wagon and load us up with more food, bottles of wine, a bucket of mussels. We carry everything up the steep stairs to our house, which is on stilts like all the other houses this far down Dune Road.

My father mixes stingers or gimlets for the women, scotch on the rocks and martinis for the men. Ed Madigan and Jim O'Brien fight over the grill, arguing about when to put the steaks and the corn on. Dizzy drools at their feet. Libby Madigan, Katie O'Brien, and Sissy Farinello recline in deck chairs and smoke. My mother swirls between her guests, chatting and laughing with the men, or sitting for a moment next to Sissy and taking a puff off her cigarette. But she never sits down for long. She gathers empty glasses and hands them off to my father for refills.

Johnny Farinello is in the kitchen wearing my mother's apron, wooden spoon in hand. He stands over a steaming pot of mussels, tosses in handfuls of parsley and douses them with white wine and the olive oil his family imports. Careful not to spill it, I bring him a martini and ask if the mussels are ready. He takes the drink from me and tousles my hair. He calls me bambina and tells me they're not mussels, they're cozze.

"Okay," I say, "So when can we eat the … cozy?"

"Quinn, honey."

My mother comes up beside us. Her bracelet jingles and I can smell her too-sweet perfume, Fracas, as she leans over me to take a look. "A work of art requires patience."

I join Patrick along with John Jr., Toby Madigan, Erin and Matty O'Brien who are doing their best to annoy everybody. We run back and forth on the deck, climbing up on the railing and jumping off to see who can make the loudest crash. When my father's record skips he shoos us all down to the beach. We toss off our sandals and run along the sandy path. Further down the shore we find an abandoned lifeguard's chair. John Jr. suggests jumping off that instead. Patrick and Toby are the biggest, so they go first. They leap into the air, arms flailing, and land with a thud in the sand.

"No way," Patrick says, when it's my turn.

He tells me I'm too small, which comes as a great relief.

"Next year." He takes my hand and we walk down to the water till it is time for dinner.

The mothers pile our plates with food and we scramble for seats. The cornhusks are charred on the outside, but they pull off easily in silky strands. We slather the steaming ears in butter and salt while they are still too hot to eat. Patrick shows me how to wedge the mussels apart with my fingers and scoop them out with a fork. They look like little tangerine tongues inside black shell mouths.

We eat until we're stuffed, until there is barely room for Katie O'Brien's Key Lime Pie. After dessert Libby Madigan wants to dance. Toby makes a face, embarrassed, when his mother kicks off her mules and hoists Jim O'Brien out of his chair. The music gets turned up louder and louder until only Libby Madigan's squealie laugh can be heard over it. Then they are all dancing, so we dance, too, in jerky movements, making fun. My father lifts me up and I wrap my legs around his waist and we sway back and forth as the sun sinks lower and lower into the Atlantic, disappears.

It's late when I wake up. Maybe I fell asleep sitting on my mother's lap while she and Sissy shared another cigarette and whispered to one another. By then I was already in my pajamas. Or maybe it was beside Patrick and John Jr. on the sofa and my father carried me up to my room, snugging the covers around me.

I thought I heard voices, a car. The Farinellos just leaving? I tiptoe down to the kitchen, but nobody's there. The counters are thick with dirty plates, cigarettes crushed out in cold food. I walk outside. The deck chairs are zigzagged along the railing. One is tipped over. Cocktail glasses and smoldering ashtrays are scattered everywhere. From the speakers there is only the scratch of the needle at the end of a record as it skips over and over.

I go back up and check my parents' room. Nobody. I cross the hall and peer into Patrick's. He's asleep with Dizzy on the bed beside him.

When I start to pull the door closed he wakes up. "Quinn?"

"Where is everybody?"

"I don't know. I fell asleep." Dizzy leaps off the bed, wagging and licking my feet. Patrick gets up and rubs his eyes.

The moon is a thin, distant curve of light in the dark sky. The air is wet and the tide is crashing in, filling up almost half of the beach. We climb down the worn wooden stairs and walk barefoot through the dunes into the pale sand.

Dizzy runs up ahead of us and disappears in the fog.

"Creepy," I say.

"Maybe they went over to Madigans'."

We walk past the other houses, all on stilts like ours. Against the night sky they look eerie and fragile, like little squirrel nests perched in the highest branches of bare trees.

When we get to Madigans' it's obvious they're sleeping. Not a single light.

"Come on," Patrick says, turning back.

"Maybe we should knock."

"It's cold. Let's go."

Back at our place Patrick lifts the needle from the record and shuts it off. He starts doing the dishes. I'm not tall enough to reach the sink, so I carry all the glasses inside and dump the ashtrays into the trash. I give Dizzy a steak bone and she settles with great content in front of the doorway, gnawing.

Patrick washes and rinses the silverware and plates, lining everything up on a yellow and white dishtowel that he's laid out on the counter like my mother does. Then he washes the glasses placing them in neat rows beside the plates and leaving the pots and pans in the sink to soak. I sit at the table with my knees hugged up to my chest up and my nightgown pulled down over my feet. I want to tell Patrick that I'm afraid, but I don't say anything because he doesn't say anything.

In the morning, our father is quiet. We walk with him down to our beach and along the shoreline. Tan legs in motion. Waves slapping our feet and splashing our shins, feet digging into the sand and leaving footprints to fill with water and melt away with the tide. A long way down, we see a woman fishing. She has long silvery-blonde hair and big breasts. Her hands are rough and brown. Her hands look older than the rest of her. We'd seen her so many mornings, if we hadn't, if I had just passed her on the street in town, I never would have pictured her fishing in that orange tank suit.

We watch her with a pull on her line. She fights with the fish, finally reeling it in. It's a young shark, struggling and twisting, making grooves in the sand. She holds it steady, works the hook from its mouth and lifts it easily, tossing it back into the surf. Without another glance she baits her line and sits in her chair. My dad calls out good morning and she nods. He loves to fish, too, but can never convince any of us to spend a day with him in his boat, drifting the bay.

We walk so long and so far he has to carry me. He scoops me up onto his back, pulling my arms around him. Patrick runs ahead of us, as usual gathering shells along the waterline, circling back and holding them up for our approval. Patrick is always smiling, his long hair curling like a girl's studied ringlets. Once he was towheaded, but each year grows a bit darker, gold streaks glinting in the light. My hair's cut short, in a pixie, which I hate. As we walk, the haze begins to burn off along the shore and the sky comes into focus. When we get home our mother is up on the deck in her tennis skirt reading the paper, blue-green hydrangeas blooming in terra cotta pots around her.

Jerry the cat reappears, circling my leg. I pick him up and he's already purring. The phone has rung about twenty times. With the curtains pulled closed, I'm starting to feel claustrophobic. The air is dense, the room over-warm. We're still hunched around Mandy's battered formica table, the two of them weighing out ounces and grams, funneling the coke into glass vials or spooning it into snow seals.

I've been folding seals from Mandy's magazines, enough to supply an entire dorm it seems. I will be folding and creasing them in my sleep. That is, if I ever manage to sleep. I'm losing track of time. The phone rings again. Nobody even mentions it. My hand shakes as I reach for my 100th cigarette.

My mother's got a Parliament burning in the ashtray on the counter, the phone between her shoulder and chin while she tries to unwind the long yellow cord from its tangled spiral and stretch it across the kitchen.

"Who's that?" I point to the man with the clipboard in the dining room.

"The mover," she says. "He's doing an estimate."

"What's that?"

"To tell us how much it costs. No more questions."

I always bug her when she is on the phone.

"Chicago," she says into the receiver.

"Who are you talking to?"

"Sissy. Now go outside," she tells me "Play."

I open the door to the basement, and clunk down the stairs instead. I find Jessie ironing my father's shirts and watching her favorite soap *Dark Shadows*. Jessie drives a huge white Impala convertible. She lets me sit on her lap and steer to the end of our street. She smokes unfiltered Camels and drinks Coca-Cola out of the bottle, one after the last. I don't know where Jessie lives or what she does when she's not here, but the three days a week that she is here, I rush home to see her when the school bus drops us on the corner. Sometimes she stays late if my parents need her to and these nights are the best. She cooks us dinner—Southern food, she calls it—and then we go out for a drive with the top down. Motown blaring from the radio. She even lets Dizzy come.

"What's Chicago?" I ask her.

She doesn't remove her eyes from the television, only answering when the commercial comes on.

"Barnabus. I knew it!" She nods at the screen. "Now, what's that?"

"Chicago," I say.

"It's a city in Illinois. You all are moving there."

"Moving?"

"For your father's job."

"Are you coming?"

"No, baby-cakes. I've got my own children to look after."

I start crying instantly. "You've got kids?"

"Of course I do."

And then I cry even harder. I run back upstairs to my mother who is walking around, pointing at pieces of furniture while the man with the clipboard jots things down.

In the evening when our father comes in from the train, we've already been sitting at the table for over an hour. Waiting. Fidgeting. He puts his briefcase down on my mother's desk chair and walks to the bar, pours himself a scotch then leans against the counter. My mother fills four plates. She sits down and scoots her chair close to the table. Patrick and I slurp our milk and push our food around with our forks. I try passing some green beans under the table to Diz, but even she won't eat them.

"Don't feed the dog," he says.

"Aren't you going to eat?" Patrick asks.

"I'll eat when I'm good goddamned ready—"

"—Tom,"

"Why are we moving to Chicago?" I ask.

"Your father's been promoted. Isn't that great?" She tells us we'll have a new house, a better house, with lots of trees and a pond.

"You mean there's no ocean?"

"Of course not," Patrick says.

"How do you know?"

"Because I know."

"That's my son," my father says. "The know it all."

A few weeks later, Sissy and my mother sit on the living room floor with a thick sheaf of paper and bundles of brown tape. They are wrapping up everything, picture frames and paperweights, silver candlesticks. Huge cardboard boxes rest along the wall, marked with thick black marker. Kitchen, den, patio. Every so often one of them bursts into tears and they lean over and hug each other.

Upstairs, Patrick is in his room listening to music. He's got all his 45s around him. A large green apple stamped at the center of the vinyl.

"Trick?"

"Yeah?"

"Will we still go to the beach?"

"I guess. I don't know."

"I don't want to go."

"Me too," he says.

His bed is stripped down to the mattress and all the dresser drawers are pulled out, resting empty beside it, clothing already in boxes. Patrick starts gathering up the 45s into a neat stack, arranging the cardboard sleeves so they all face the same direction.

A record drops from the arm onto the turntable and begins to spin.

"Last one," Patrick says.

A car door slams and then another. Mandy jumps up and goes to answer. I watch him from the kitchen. He opens the front door slightly, peering out, the safety slung across to the doorframe as before, an absurd formality, given the flimsiness of the chain. "Get in here," he says, then goes through the same ritual of shutting the door, unlocking the lock, and opening it again.

"Patrick, man, we've been looking for you."

Scotty comes in with Nadine who immediately plops onto my brother's lap and kisses him, lots of tongue.

"Nice to see you, too, Nadine," Mandy tells her.

But Nadine is already eyeing the drugs, dipping her finger into one of the piles and rubbing the coke over her gums. "Wicked," she says.

Scotty pulls a handful of Quaaludes from his pocket and dumps them on the table.

"Biscuit, anyone?"

"Maybe we should go out."

They all look at me as if I've suggested something obscene.

"Mandy no go out," Mandy says. "But Sister's bored watching us jones."

Nadine glares at me, "It's not even half nine."

Patrick studiously avoids my gaze.

Scotty pushes the pills aside and busies himself rolling a joint.

After our parents back out of the driveway and we can see their taillights heading up the street, we cut through the opening in the hedge that divides our yard from Spit's. We don't ring the bell because Mr. and Mrs. Spitzer are out of town and we know Spit is down in his kingdom, the basement.

The room is smoky with patchouli incense and pot. I climb onto Spit's waterbed. It gurgles and ripples. There are posters on all the walls. One of them says 'Stoned Again.' It's broken up into panels, cartoony-drawings of a man's face, eyes that pop out over a bulbous nose and an elongated chin, tangerine and lime in the glow of the blacklight. In each section the face gets more and more distorted, until the last, where his head is completely melted and only the eyeballs bulge from a pool of swirled fluorescent colors.

Spit makes me practice rolling fake joints with a No. 2 pencil and Bambú papers that come in a thin packet with beige stripes, kind of like those tissues for wiping your eyeglasses. Patrick and Spit buy pot from some fraternity guy at the university in the next town over. Patrick says DU stands for Drugs Unlimited. I twist the rolling papers around the pencil while Spit air-guitars to Hendrix and Patrick cleans all the seeds out of the pot. Eventually Spit tosses the bag over to me. With a magazine open on my lap, I sprinkle the weed into the papers, trying to be careful. It was a lot smoother going with the pencil, but when I finish, I hold up the joint and they both seem pleased.

Lisa Spitzer is a cheerleader. Any chance she gets, she'll parade around in her cheerleading skirt. She marches down the basement stairs and glares at us from the doorway.

"Just wait till Mom and Dad get back."

"Why don't you go bleach your hair some more?"

"Eddie!" She yells. Then she focuses in on me. "What do you hang around with these burnouts for? Do you want to end up like those Tech girls with a motorhead boyfriend and hickeys on your neck?"

I don't really know what she means, but I know it's an insult. Lisa is always talking about how she and her boyfriend Farland are applying to Ivy League schools. Spit and Patrick call him Fartland, but only to Lisa, not to his face. I think they actually like Farland. It's Lisa they despise.

"Fuck you, Lisa," Patrick says. "Quinn's a photographer."

"Yeah, right. Art school."

Scotty and I head up to the 7-11 to buy more beer and cigarettes. The air has an edge to it, a reminder that winter isn't necessarily over. To me the night air is bliss, the crisp outline of the trees along the parkway just beginning to bloom, the mountains etched against a lapis sky in the distance.

As we walk, he recounts a story about road tripping to a show. Something about a speeding ticket in Nevada. Anything that has to do with the Dead is tedious to me. I know he's just trying to be nice. Scotty—and now Mandy—are my brother's only friends who haven't tried to sleep with me. For that alone, I like them. But Scotty is the last person Patrick should share a house with. He's got too much money and too much time. Always taking just one more semester off.

When we get back, we follow Mandy back into the cramped kitchen, still in our jackets. He puts the beer in the fridge then turns and looks at the stack of seals and vials we've sorted. "It wouldn't hurt to unload some of this shit before we do it all ourselves."

Patrick removes Nadine from his lap and stands up. "Right," he says. "Little Women."

Nadine groans at the name of the band.

Mandy reaches over to touch my arm. "Stop by any time, Little Sister."

"One for the road?" Scotty passes out downers like candy. Everybody takes one but me.

Nadine scoops up the helmet I'd worn on the ride over and without so much as a word, I've been relegated to Scotty's Jeep. I don't want my brother driving his motorcycle. And I definitely don't want to get into a vehicle with Scotty, but I know if I stay in this kitchen a year might pass, so I follow him, climb in, and fasten my seatbelt. I roll down my window while Scotty fiddles with the cassette player.

"I'll see you at the club, okay?" Patrick says.

But his gaze is looking past me.

I've spent the whole day and now much of the evening waiting for him to really look at me. Waiting for some moment when we would actually talk. I took the bus down here to see him. Spent the whole ride preparing a speech I'll never give, some conversation I pretended we'd have that I'm too chicken shit to bring up, but even if I did—what? I'd save him? He'd save me? Is that what I'm hoping for?

And the fucking bus.

I hadn't been out here two months before Patrick borrowed my car and totaled it, wrapping it round a power pole and abandoning it there. The story goes that he left it in the driveway with the keys still in the ignition. A family trait. Somebody nicked it and crashed it.

And maybe it really was like that.

Who knows?

Who cares?

I don't care about the fucking car.

I just want my brother back.

In the springtime I walk through my brother's bedroom, running my fingers along the walls and looking at his things. A tiger-striped blanket on his bed, spread of albums on the floor, oversized headphones plugged into the amp. There's a poster of Bobby Hull making a slap shot and a Bob Marley T-shirt slung over an antique wicker chair, rolls of black tape, and his white Adidas, green stains around the edges from mowing lawns during summer.

The bookshelves are lined with a complete set of the Hardy Boys mysteries that our grandparents gave him. The blue spines are numbered just like my Nancy Drew series, only Nancy's are bright yellow. I pretend that Patrick and I are like those young sleuths, always caught up in some twisted narrative where we are the only ones who can solve everything. There are other books, too, from his high school English classes. I never saw him reading them, but I'd memorized the titles—*Great Expectations*, *In Our Time*, *The Stranger*—pulling them from the shelves and reading them, myself, then returning them, careful to keep them alphabetized as he had done.

I grab the hockey puck off his dresser. I like the weight of it in my palm. I carry it over and sit cross-legged beside the stereo, pull his albums in and out of their paper sleeves, scanning lyrics. Using only my palms to hold the edges, like Patrick showed me, I lift Sticky Fingers off the turntable and slip it into its zippered-cover. I replace it with *Dark Side of the Moon*. The sound of the cash register at the beginning of "Money."

I spend a long time in the sleeping porch off of his room. Taking my camera from around my neck, I rest the lens right up on the glass and stare out through the viewfinder at the cluster of lean leafless magnolia trees, branches encased in ice. I am waiting for the furry ovals to muster the strength to shed their skins and blossom, white and pink and sweet. They seem to blink and shiver, watery eyes shut tight near the pale white skin of the bark. But the tiny buds won't open. Not with me watching.

When he comes home, Patrick always heads straight for the sunroom, just below where I'm standing. I don't like that room. Even with all those windows I don't recall it ever being sunny or warm. There's a fountain sunk into one corner, statue of a little boy astride a dolphin, water streaming from the mouth of the fish, the splash of water funneling into the pool below. The floors surrounding the fountain are made from ceramic tiles. Our mom says they are from Venice, a city surrounded by water. The tiles are a dark red-brown, as dark as dried blood.

From upstairs, I hear the television switch on and I picture Patrick spreading over the sofa, red-eyed and quiet. I stare at the magnolia for a few more minutes. When my wrists begin to ache from the weight of the camera, I wander downstairs to look for him.

Early one evening when the thaw has lifted and the days have begun to stretch longer, I find Patrick in the driveway, his army-green pack slung over his shoulder. He seems startled when I come up beside him.

"I need to hide this," he says. "Now."

I suggest the bat houses, a bit elaborate maybe, but right out of a mystery story. There's an extension ladder in the garage for climbing up on the roof to clear leaves from the gutters when they get clogged. Patrick and I carry it across the yard and prop it up alongside the tall tower of a bat house. Built at the turn of the century, our sprawling house was designed with this feature to keep the mosquitos and other insects away. Cocktail parties on the lawn in summer. And we still have bats—swooping low in the sky at dusk when the weather grows warm. During the winter we forget about them.

I hold the bottom as steady as I can and watch his feet move above me from one rung to the next, staring up at the frayed edges of his Levi's, the muddy bottoms of his shoes. He is about six feet high when I get scared.

"Maybe you should come down."

He just laughs.

"What if they bite you?"

"They're still sleeping," he tells me. "Don't you watch vampire movies?"

"Trick, I'm serious."

He keeps climbing, boy-scout pack full of weed strapped to his shoulders.

We hear our mother's squeaky brakes as she pulls into the driveway. Maybe Patrick panicked and lost his footing. Or maybe I jiggled the ladder. I'm not sure. But I see his body slowly falling backward. Patrick falling. Then the ladder falling. I have to run to get out of the way. It seems like it should make a huge crash, but it's more of a thud, a stifled scream when my brother's body hits the ground, the ladder tumbling down on top of him.

He lies on his side, his arm crushed beneath him. I can see the bone sticking out at an angle. There's blood. I start crying.

"Take my pack."

"What?"

"Help me get it off."

I just stand there crying.

"Quinn, get your shit together," he says.

I lean down beside him, pulling his good arm through the strap, then disentangle the broken one. He lets out a little gasp when I touch it, struggling to pull himself up.

"Just hide it."

"What about your arm?"

The car door slams and we hear our mother's singsong call, "Anybody home?"

"Go!"

I get up and start running and I don't look back.

The old Ellis place is an empty mansion a few blocks over. Kids are always daring one another to climb in through the broken basement window. I've never taken the dare. That house with its emptiness and its damp dark frightens me. I run around the side and climb under the back porch where Spit and the older boys smoke cigarettes or joints. I unbuckle the backpack and look inside.

It's not pot, but cocaine. I'm not sure how I even know it is cocaine. But I do know. I hold it up noticing the way the white powder fogs the insides of the plastic bag. I pull the zipper apart and stick my finger inside. In the movies, the drug dealers always taste the drugs to see if they are good. I lick my finger; it tastes a bit like chlorine. I have no idea where to put the bag, but I can't leave it here.

The last light of the day infuses everything with an almost infrared glow as I climb out from under the porch. Honeysuckle blooms orange along the trellis. I pluck one and coax the juice from the flower to get the bitter taste out of my mouth. Overhead, in the trees, the locusts seem to scream. Usually their cries make me want to run, but tonight

I take my time, hyper conscious of the weight of the pack, and let the chorus of noise wash over me.

When I get home my mother's car is gone. No doubt to the hospital. The streetlamps blink on as I stand looking at the long slope of our roof. Two bats skitter low in the air and disappear. Set back behind the house, our garage has a small apartment above it where Patrick helped me set up my darkroom. My mom says the apartment used to be for the chauffeur, back when people had them. Why didn't we just hide it here in the first place? Why did I have to go all Nancy Drew with the bat houses? I shove the bag of coke in an empty drum for developing film and put it in the cabinet behind some boxes of Ilford paper.

Back down in the yard, I kneel beside the ladder on the damp ground, ripping out the blades of grass where Patrick's blood had splattered. I clutch the grass in my fist, trying not to cry. I stay there for a long time, finally fling it all into the darkness and drag the ladder back to the garage.

A couple days later Patrick is released from the hospital. His surgery was complicated and long. His shoulder dislocated, the forearm broken, and his wrist shattered. When he comes home, he has both a cast and a sling. He gives me a look and I try to smile to let him know I did what he asked me to, that he doesn't need to worry. Nobody says so, but it is understood that he will never play on the hockey team again. Even so, some part of me still thinks this is all just a game. That Patrick and I are the good guys.

The next day, he finds me in my darkroom. He's holding a duffle bag, setting it down to lock the door after Dizzy trails in behind him.

"Where is it?"

I know what he means, but I get anxious all over again, as I did beneath the porch of the Ellis mansion. I go into my closet-darkroom and find the metal canister.

"Good girl."

He locks the door then sits down, unzipping the bag with his good hand and pulling out some sports equipment, an old hockey helmet and a baseball glove, then a small scale that he sets on the table. I don't know what to say or do. I pretend to go back and check on my prints, poking them with the wooden tongs in the wash and flipping the images over, but he calls after me to turn on some music.

"And not that Top 40 crap," he says.

I know he's teasing me to make me calm down. I switch the radio over to FM and spin the knob down to the end of the dial, finding the college station. Roxy Music.

"Both ends burning," Patrick says and laughs. "Bring me that photo, okay?"

"Why?"

"I want to show you something."

One of the first shots I was really proud of was Dune Road in the early morning, the beach houses on stilts lining both sides of the road. Our mother loved that one. She and my father had it framed for me, although it never ended up being hung in the house. I lift the frame from the wall and hand it to Patrick. He lays it flat on the coffee table next to the scale. Unable to open the plastic bag, he holds it up. "Help me out here?"

I sit beside him and open it. I'm trying not to stare at the white powder, some of it in chunks, the rest of it smooth and heavy in the corners of the bag.

"You know what this is, don't you?"

"Yeah." Did I know? I thought I knew. "I tasted it."

"You did?" He's laughing, but then he stops. "Thanks for taking care of it, by the way." He asks me to scoop a bit of the coke out onto the scale and starts giving me instructions how to weigh it.

"This is vitamin B," he uses his cast to point at a brown glass jar. "To cut it."

I nod like I know what he means.

"Taste a little bit of it, too, so you know the difference."

I touch the dust inside the lid from the jar.

"The texture's different." He explains that adding the vitamin B is how you make a profit. "But you never want to step on it too much. Just enough."

Patrick teaches me how to slice the corners from the pages of an old *National Geographic* to make snow seals and how to crease the square of paper diagonally, spoon the coke into the crease and fold the corners around it.

"You can tell, see?" he says. "This is a quarter. And this is a half. And this is a gram. If you think you're going to forget which is which then write it on the seal, but you should always be able to tell just from the size."

While he is talking he scrapes the coke back and forth over my photo with the razor, chopping up some of the chunks and making little piles, his broken arm limp in its sling.

"Now you try it," he holds out the razor. "Be careful, okay?"

I like this part, the chopping and arranging. The white rocks have a rosy tone, a flakiness like the mica we studied in science class.

"It's kind of pink."

"Peruvian. Now smooth it out into lines."

"Like this?"

"Yeah, good," he says. "I'm going to show you something else— mostly because I'd rather show you myself than have some asshole my age get you drunk and try to feed you lines. You're old enough, you know? My friends are even starting to look at you."

I'm embarrassed. I try to figure out a way to ask him which friend he means without being too obvious. "What are you talking about?"

"I'm just saying. Next year you'll be in high school, and the year after that, I won't be around to watch out for you."

I cannot imagine Patrick leaving. Can't picture living alone in that big house listening to our parents fight without him there. I know what he means about me getting older, but I don't want to think about that either. He hands me a twenty-dollar bill and asks me to roll it up tight. The bill is crisp and new and I start curling the long edge of it.

"Q—" He smiles. "Other way."

"Just checking to see if you're paying attention," I say. I flip the twenty, re-rolling it into a narrow tube. He takes it and lowers himself down, trying not to knock into the glass with his broken arm, and I hear him sniffing.

"This is hard to do one-handed. Usually you plug the other side of your nose with your finger." He offers me the rolled bill out and tells me I can try it, but only if I want to.

I always wanted to be just like him, wearing Levi's and skating fast in hockey skates. There was no way I'd let him think I was still a little girl. I grab it and lean over my photograph, noticing the reflection of my face in the glass, the image underneath and the white lines like streams of sand dividing the road where the two of us used to play.

If Mandy's kitchen was scary, Scotty's driving is scarier. But at least there's air. For a moment, I'm reminded of Dizzy, the way she'd climb over me and lean as much of her body as possible out of the window to feel the rush of wind in her face. I'd like to do that, but I'm petrified as it is. I close my eyes, but that's worse. I smoke instead, keeping a close watch on the distance of the brake lights ahead of us, arcs of light from the intermittent streetlamps along the dark road.

Scotty pulls his Jeep in front of a fire hydrant and stumbles out. We walk past abandoned buildings toward the club. A crowd lingers nearby, listening to the band without paying the cover. Scotty greets the Rasta at the door. He doesn't charge us, just puts a plastic wristband on me, as if he's checking me into surgery.

The Merc is a sprawling windowless warehouse with a stage at the back in an open cavern of space, a bar and cafe when you first walk in. A few people sit at mismatched vintage tables or on low sofas along the perimeter of the cafe. Some stand at the bar ordering drinks, but almost everyone is trying to lock down real estate in front of the stage. We lean our elbows on the bar. And Scotty really does need to lean on it. I can't believe he drove. Or that I rode with him. The bartender pours two shots of tequila. Scotty promptly puts a gram into the bartender's shirt pocket. I ask for water.

"You don't want the shot?"

I shake my head.

They pour salt on their wrists, lick it off, and gulp down the tequila, grimacing as they suck on lime wedges. The bartender fills a pint glass with ice and water for me and tells me his name, which I don't catch.

"This is Patrick's sister," Scotty says. "Take care of her."

I don't think I can talk. I've been clenching my teeth for so long that my mouth feels wired shut. But the reggae is soothing and slow and even though I'm not any less stranded here than I was at Mandy's, I start breathing normally, or as normally as I can considering, and I only consumed a fraction of what has been on offer. I don't know what I thought I would accomplish this weekend. I'm an asshole for partying with Patrick. I came down here to talk to him, not to do an eightball together. Remorse floods my senses like the aftertaste of so many lines.

"Hey Photo Girl, I thought that was you."

Instinctively, I feel inside my bag for my Leicaflex, relieved to find it. When we left Patrick's house it was supposedly just a quick run over to Mandy's. Who knows when I might have seen it again? But I've learned to never leave it behind.

"Shasta."

"C'est moi."

He wraps his arms around me. I try to remember the last time anyone hugged me. I usually shy away from such things. But Shasta is Shasta. We met the first week of classes in a mix-up when the university assigned me to be his roommate on an all-male floor of the dorm. He's your basic trustafarian. One of many in these parts. He's solid though. And sweet. Always inviting me to his family's place in Aspen even though I never accept.

"If your bro shows up, ask him if he'll trade some of that pristine pink for my totally kind Shasta bud." His head swivels back and forth like one of those dashboard hula dancers. I tell him he's easier to understand when he speaks French. He waves Kim over and we watch him take long strides through the crowd. Kim looks a bit like a Nordic Jesus. Tall and thin and all angles. He towers over Shasta and me.

"So this is where you hide."

"Tonight, anyway."

The boys chatter a bit until I realize they are talking about me. Shasta nudges Kim. "Have you ever seen her pics?"

Kim says he hasn't, but he'd be happy to model for me. I know he's kidding, but I would like to make a portrait of him. When we were kids, Patrick was my muse, suffering my early experiments, standing in awkward poses for hours, listing into and out of the light or surrendering himself to shadows. Allowing me to frame and reframe him. Again and again. He tolerated the learning curve of each new format, always encouraging me to photograph other people.

Since I can remember, the architecture of the face and the landscape of the body have meant more to me than a skyline or an object ever could. A portrait collapses time. It blurs the margin between public and private space. Allowing me to connect with people in a way that, otherwise, I never could. In its silence, a portrait can contain the echo of conversations past. Perhaps in the best of them, a sibylline glimpse of what lies ahead. How had Patrick known a camera would suit me? Or was it just luck? He does seem to know things. But then, he doesn't have the problem of feeling apart. Or never seems to. Everyone gravitates to him—and they always have. Even when we were children. By the time he was in his teens, it seemed whatever quality you most desired, he could sense it and was able to reassure you that you radiated it. Without ever saying a word. Beside him you feel your most clever, most beautiful, most talented. Your best self.

I don't have that ability. Sometimes I manage a sliver of it when I'm making a picture. With my camera I can move closer. It brings me inside. Without it I don't have the same access. Or so I always thought. But earlier today, looking at the images Patrick chose to pack and bring with him, moments from our childhood that I had documented, I realized this is actually false. I was never really inside.

There are almost no photographs of the two of us together.

Even fewer of the whole family including me.

As if I were never there.

Patrick gives me a Kodak Instamatic for my seventh birthday. Maybe he didn't buy it, but I know it was his idea. We take the camera outside on the deck and he shows me how to load the film. He makes sure the back of the camera is properly shut and hands it to me.

"Shoot, cowboy."

Holding the viewfinder up to my eye it's as if whatever I look at can be mine. I can have any moment I choose. This moment. Or the one just after. Photography is a trick. I carry the Instamatic with me everywhere. Click. Click. Click. In the morning sun I walk up and down Dune Road making pictures. Passing cars press shells into the sticky asphalt, a brilliant mosaic. I kneel down close and examine the macadam through my viewfinder.

Click.

I drop another roll of film into the belly of the camera and wedge the used film into my pocket. A tiny seaplane passes overhead, motor sputtering. It drags an ad for Coppertone, the banner fluttering behind the plane. Image of a girl in green bikini bottoms, a little brown dog tugging her swimming suit between his teeth, her fair skin beneath it exposed.

The beach is empty as I climb along the slippery rock bridge of the jetty, to the tip, and dangle my feet over the edge. The ocean is dark gray-blue, then white, as it breaks into frothy swirls against the dark rocks. Looking east there is only sea and sky, no boats on the horizon. I photograph the water rising up around me.

Each day, with the help of the Instamatic, I see things I hadn't noticed before. I never grow tired of photographing the beach, but I soon realize I have a knack for making pictures of people. Patrick, always. My mother in her leopard bikini. My father wearing his thick black-framed glasses. I snap so many pictures that everyone starts to mumble. No. Not now. Stop.

The summer passes as it does, in cloudless skies and great tumbling waves. High tide. Low tide. With each day I begin to notice how the light changes. How shadows tend to point south, how they were smaller when I first got my camera and how over time they seem to stretch just a bit longer. I make pictures in earnest all through the summer. Soon we will go back to our real house and then we start school.

After a long day riding the surf and playing with friends, Patrick and I weave through the dunes on our way home. My brother looks back over his shoulder to check on me, green eyes and freckled shoulders, tall grass blowing around him, the curve of picket fence to hold the dunes in place, half buried in sand and tilting.

"Wait," I tell him. "I want a picture."

He says we should hurry, but I make one anyway. Then run after him.

When I look up, I see our father at the railing of our deck. As we get closer, I notice he has a drink in his hand. Just the way he holds onto the glass tells me he's drunk. If there's booze in it, he never sets it down, tan fingers cupping the rim.

"You're late."

"But it's not even dinner time."

"You and that damn camera," he says.

"Sorry, Dad," Patrick says, "my fault."

"You kids—everything I do is for this family."

"Here we go," I whisper to Patrick as we climb the steps.

"Who pays the bills, who takes you on trips—"

"Dad, what's wrong?" Patrick says.

"I'll tell you what's wrong. You're goddamn late. No beach tomorrow."

"But we only have two more days to swim," Patrick says. It isn't a protest so much as a statement of fact.

"And you can spend them in the house."

Aunt Mary is watching from the window. "Ah, Tom, they're just kids," she calls.

"Who asked you?" His voice a growl we shrink from.

We slink across the deck toward the back door and open it, but my father grabs Patrick by the shoulder and yanks him around, smashing his face into the screen. "Did you hear me?" Patrick's cheek and nose are scraped, an accordion of skin crumpled back. Pale underneath, as if the bone is showing through. Blood comes rushing up. He bolts up the stairs and Dizzy and I chase after, but he's slammed his door before we reach the landing. Dizzy sits perplexed and whining outside his room.

My mother is lying on her bed in a matching beige bra and underwear. She's wearing a sleeping mask—like the lone ranger's but without the holes. My aunt is still by the window. She turns and looks at me.

"Mom—."

"Better get dressed, we've got reservations at the club." She lifts the mask slightly then lets it fall back over her eyes.

"Dad hit Patrick."

"Go get cleaned up," she says. This time she doesn't even lift the mask.

"Aunt Mary even saw him."

My aunt turns from the window, offering me a weak smile.

"And no cutoffs—a skirt," my mother says.

"Your mother has a headache," Aunt Mary says. "Why don't I help you find something to put on?"

Later, when I develop the film, there is Patrick, tan and smiling, our beach house ever precarious on its stilts and the shadowy figure of our father looming in the background.

Across the crowded bar I see Patrick and Nadine beelining through the crowd. Shasta and Kim notice them too and send me after on a mission. In the bathroom, two girls in long tie-dye skirts stand beside the sink, one braiding the other's hair. They eye me in the mirror as I come in. Patrick's shoes are visible underneath the stall door.

"Trick, it's me."

"Get in here," he says, imitating Mandy. The door opens and I squeeze inside. Nadine's straddling the toilet backward, scraping out lines with a credit card and snorting them off the tank. A practice only cocaine could induce. Especially in someone like Nadine. Patrick reaches over to hold her hair out of the way.

"Fancy some?"

"I'm good."

She's my height. Dark everything. The opposite of me. Posh accent from growing up abroad. I want to hate her. But I can't. She hasn't been around long enough to blame for any of this. When she finishes, Patrick hands me one of the glass vials he and Mandy filled, then thinks better of it and gives me two. I ask him how much, but he just waves me off. Standing this close, his skin looks gray, his cheeks hollow. He still has the appearance of someone attractive but the lustre is gone. As close as we are I can't reach him. I don't even know how to try.

"I love a spring snowstorm," Nadine says.

"Who doesn't?" Patrick swaps places with her.

I've been nagging our mother all winter and now that it is nearly over, she finally agrees to buy me skates like my brother's. I feel triumphant abandoning my pointy white figure skates and clomping around the store on the thick steel blades.

She shakes her head, "All right, so no figure skating. How about ballet?"

"No way," I say. "Too pansy."

"I suppose this is what I deserve, naming you after your grandfather."

"And Aunt Mary," I remind her. "Mary Quinn."

"Your aunt is a tomboy, too. I should have known."

That afternoon, Patrick and I hike down the hill through the woods behind our house. My father and Mr. Spitzer take turns clearing the snow off the pond because it edges up on both our properties. A lot of neighborhood kids come down here, but we like it best when there's nobody but us. Or maybe just Eddie. Today Spit is already here, sitting on a large log, smoking a joint. Patrick and I creep up behind him as quiet as we can.

"Shit!" he says. "I thought you were my dad."

Patrick looks at the joint then at me.

"She won't tell—will you, Quinn?" Spit blows a smoke ring into the cold air. "You're not like my snitch sister, always getting me grounded."

I shake my head.

"Speaking of which," he says. "Curfew."

He offers Patrick the joint, but Patrick says he has to practice. We watch him walk back through the snow as we put on our skates. Patrick pulls my laces tight, looping them twice around the backs of my ankles and patting each foot when he's finished.

"Okay?"

"Good." I get up and wobble down to the pond.

Patrick practices his slap shot in the lone net that's set up. I go round and round getting used to the weight of my new skates and crossing one foot over the other on the turns, just like he taught me.

I switch directions and circle the other way, loving the shush of the blades cutting into the ice. The trees are huge, especially the oaks, snow-bent branches catching the last of the sun and sparkling. Even though I'm cold, the light reminds me of the beach, the way it gleams on the wet rocks of the jetty. Patrick glides up and does a hockey stop just in front of me. He grabs both of my hands, turns and starts skating backwards, fast, pulling me after him.

The crowd seems to have doubled in the few minutes we were in the bathroom. The band's signature sound is upbeat, ecstatic even, and belies everything I'm feeling. I tell my brother I've got a lift home to Boulder. I haven't even asked Shasta yet, but I'm banking on a ride. Patrick says he thought I was spending the weekend with him. I lie and say I have to study. I can't tell if he's bummed or relieved. He offers to drive me back in the morning instead, that way we can still have brunch together.

"Let's do it next weekend."

"Time for a bevvy then," Nadine says, "Cheers."

And with that I'm dismissed.

But Patrick turns back and says, "Have a drink with us before you go."

When we get to the bar, Shasta actually jumps with glee. I hand him a book of matches with one of the vials inside it and he slips it into a pocket.

"Magnifique."

He offers to pay Patrick or swap for some weed, but Patrick just asks him to make sure I get home safe.

"Bien sûr," he says. "But that's like totally trop généreux."

Patrick laughs and for a minute just hearing his laugh I feel better. Bless you, Shasta.

We order a round. Patrick and I both light cigarettes. Nadine is petulant, stabbing the lemon twist in her glass with a plastic stir. She's not a hippie chick and this is not her scene. We have that in common, anyway. I can't wait to leave. But now the Boulder boys each want a bump and nobody seems to be in a rush. The longest day turning into the longest night. I look down and realize I've already finished my drink.

Our parents keep the liquor in the safe, not because they want to lock it up, but because they think it's funny. The safe came with the house and happens to be near the wet bar. I'm not sure if anyone knows the combination. But in any case, it's never locked. I grab onto the handle and swing the heavy door open. I crouch down and stroke the cool glass bottles with my fingers. I read and reread all the labels. Some of the words I can make out on my own, others I just know what they are from seeing them so often.

There's a tall slender bottle with yellow liqueur inside it. I don't think anyone likes the yellow one because it is still full. The green stuff is crème de menthe. Sometimes Patrick and I have it poured over vanilla ice cream. The Canadian Club is for Mr. Spitzer and the bourbon is for my mother's friend Carol Kinney. Dick Kinney drinks gin, the one that's in the rectangular blue glass bottle. Our mother is inconsistent, one night it's a gin and tonic, the next it's a stinger. That's what the brandy is for.

There are more bottles in the other cabinets, too. My parents say the caterers open as many as possible just so they can bill them for a whole bottle. There must be six vermouths with only a little bit missing. Every time there is a party more cases arrive. On these nights my mother sits in her dressing room in front of the mirror. She pencils in her fair brows and puts on powder and lipstick, different colors depending on her dress. When she's got her face on, she teases her hair with a silver handled comb. I follow her downstairs, her perfume wafting behind her. My father will zip up the back of her dress. She straightens his tie then glides off to peek under the silver chafing dishes on the huge mahogany sideboard or to adjust the flowers in a cut-glass vase on the dining room table.

I like it when the caterers come. The young men are cute in their long white aprons and starched white shirts. They let me eat cherries by the handful while they set up the bars that are scattered throughout the house. And the kitchen is always full of people, arranging food out on trays and bustling about. The doorbell starts ringing. Everyone hugs and kisses, but carefully so no lipstick is smeared. The women always tell my mother how beautiful her house is as they slide out of their furs. Patrick and I carry the heavy coats upstairs and pile them on the bed in my parents' room. The men slap my father on the back and make their way toward the bar. They stand in a semi-circle near the bar talking about options and futures and none of it makes any sense.

Tonight, though, it's just me, rummaging around in the safe. The J&B is almost empty, but there are two full ones behind it. I lift the bottle out and unscrew the cap. I hold the bottle up to Dizzy and she backs away. Patrick says if you mix rum with juice or Coke it doesn't taste so bad. He says rum makes you happy, but scotch makes you mad, like when somebody checks you during a hockey game and you've got no choice but to fight.

I put the scotch back and look for the white label with the little bat, Bacardi. It's way in back because nobody drinks it unless it's summer. I carry the rum into the kitchen and rest it on the table in the dark. I open the refrigerator and light spills out over my slippers. I only find milk and apple juice or cranberry juice. I don't like cranberry. It's gross. I pour the rum into my favorite cup, add the apple juice and drop in some ice cubes, which makes it so full I have to sip from the edge without lifting it to avoid a big spill. At first I only taste the juice floating on top, but when it is less full I tilt the whole glass toward my mouth. It reminds me a bit of cough syrup, sweet and medicine-y when it hits the back of my throat.

The band begins its second set making it almost impossible to hear. I try to tell Patrick we're leaving but he and Nadine have friends around them and they are all moving toward the stage in one continuous wave. I call out and he looks back, smiles. I gesture to the door and he says something, but I don't catch it. He disappears into the crowd. I resolve to call him the next day. I hurry past the long queue of people near the door to look for Shasta. I see Patrick's motorcycle parked near the entrance. Just the sight of it and I start crying. I don't even know why. I wipe my eyes with the sleeve of my jacket.

I see Shasta, leaning against a mustard-colored Volvo. Vermont plates that say GR8FUL. What else? He takes one look at me and asks if I'm all right.

"Fine," I say. "I forgot something, though, could you wait a few minutes more?"

The bouncer with the dreads sees my wristband and waves me back in. I look everywhere for Patrick. An urgency bordering on panic pushes me through the crowd of people dancing. Impossibly, the reggae bass-line now sounds menacing. Faces all seem to grimace at me as I dodge limbs and lit cigarettes in an attempt to get closer to the stage. It must be the coke. Maybe that last vodka. Everything feels more drastic than it should. Even the lights are a bit too shimmery.

I don't see him anywhere. I don't even see Scotty or Nadine. I work my way back out of the crowd near the stage, scanning the area by the bar before trying the bathrooms, but he's not in either of them. I go into one of the stalls, lock the door, and bend over with my hands on my knees. I can't breathe.

I walk back out of the Merc and Patrick's motorcycle is gone.

"Fuck."

Kim saunters up. "Ready?"

I nod and ask him if he's seen my brother but he says he hasn't. He introduces me to a guy I've never seen before called Nick.

"Hey." Nick's voice is soft and low.

I don't say anything. I know I can't speak without sobbing. What the fuck is wrong with me.

Shasta's already behind the wheel, music blasting. Kim runs around to the front of the Volvo calling out, "Shotgun."

I open the back door and find half the seat is occupied by a snowboard and a small outdoor grill.

"Is that righteous or what?" Shasta asks. "I just scored it."

I don't know if he's talking about the grill or the snowboard, but either way, they are both hogging the seat. Nick and I wedge ourselves in from the other side, me in the middle, him by the door, our legs touching. Shasta and Kim fall at once into deep, but friendly, disagreement about how to get back onto the highway. Nick is quiet beside me. I sit as still as possible, tell myself not to think. I keep my eyes trained on the road. A few snowflakes in the darkness, lit up by the headlights.

I spend the whole drive facing out the window, afraid to look at my mother, afraid that looking will somehow make her cry. Or make me cry. But I don't cry. She talks most of the way, talking about anything but where we are headed and why, which makes me believe it is somehow my mother's fault. I sit there hating her for all those hours on the road. It's easier this way, easier to blame my mother for my father's condition. And she lets me blame her, lets me cling to the illusion of the perfect father, holding him up as if he were a photograph, his behavior unchanged, unchanging.

Patrick refused to make the trip with us. He's the one who had found him slumped over the wheel with the car pinning our bicycles and patio furniture against the back wall of the garage. I imagine my father on the train, making his way home from the city, the newspapers folded on his lap. The desperation that must have preceded his ordering a drink while taking Antabuse. Knowing it might kill him. Perhaps that was his wish. He gulps down a scotch just as his train pulls into the station. He stumbles from the platform to his Jaguar sedan. His face flushed, he climbs inside. Tan leather seats cool and familiar, but his heartbeat erratic, the vomit convulsing his stomach, rising up to his throat as he points the car toward home.

He isn't passed out when Patrick finds him, but clinging to the steering wheel, his chest leaning on the horn and the horn blaring, vomit all over the rosewood dash, all over his jacket and tie. Patrick screams for me to call an ambulance and I come running downstairs from my room. I had heard the car horn but ignored it, certain it was one of our neighbor's making the racket. I'll never forgive myself for this, I think, as I stand there frozen in the doorway to the garage.

"Call 911," he yells again. "Call mom."

I rush back inside and dial, answering all the operator's questions as clearly as I can. I'm not crying. Then I try to find my mother at the Racquet Club. It takes me a while to find the number because it is in her address book under T for Tennis. I can already hear the sirens by the time they answer and tell me she's already left. I put the phone down and run outside. Patrick is sitting on the floor of the garage, crying.

My mother's car pulls into the driveway just after the ambulance. She parks on the lawn. And before she's even asked what's going on, as the paramedics are lifting our father out of his car and rolling him onto the stretcher, she says, "Quinn, honey—the groceries."

I carry the heavy paper bags one by one into the kitchen and put them on the counter. The last bag is so full I almost dropped it. It is loaded with bottles of tonic, a carton of Parliaments edging out of the top. We drive in silence toward the hospital. Patrick is completely still in the front seat, tears dripping from his chin. It will be the last time I see my brother cry.

When I see my father again it is at the clinic in Minnesota. His voice has gone quiet, almost a whisper. There are no animated conversations, my eyes tracing the movements of his hands. He sits staring out the window, the world slipping by.

"Let's take a walk," I say, pulling the arm of his sweater.

We bundle on layers and go outside.

I want him to pick me up, hold me close so that I can smell the cool of his aftershave, my cheek on his neck. I wish I were six years old and that he'd carry me through the snow. Crunch of his boots cutting through the icy layer on top but he keeps his hands deep in his pockets and his head down while I struggle along behind him trying to keep up.

While we are walking it begins to snow.

Kim tugs one of Shasta's dreads then relieves him of the joint, draping it in his long thin fingers over the back of the seat, but neither of us partakes. Nick rolls down the window, but the rush of air causes that weird reverb when only one is open. With the snowboard in the way, I can't reach the other handle, so he rolls his back up. For a while nobody says anything. The tape ends, clicking over as it auto-reverses.

"Why so quiet, Photo Girl?" Shasta asks. "You must be tweaked."

Every time we hit a bump, Nick's knee knocks against mine. Normally, I'd be curious about him. I suppose I am curious about him. His hair falls in black loose curls and he's got that blue-eyes-black-eyelashes combo. Beautiful hands. I catalog all these details automatically, as I would if I were going to make a photograph of him, but at the same time I can't really focus on it.

"Long day," I say, finally.

"No doubt, dude. Your brother is a legend," Kim says.

Patrick waits for me outside the baggage claim at Stapleton, leaning on his motorcycle in a pair of faded Levis and Vuarnet sunglasses. He straps my bag to the back of his bike with a yellow bungee and hands me a helmet. The sky is high altitude blue and the sun feels warm. Until we start moving, anyway. My eyes tear up as we race down 36. Patrick drives too fast, dodging cars and leaning into the curves, the bike dips down, almost horizontal, the pavement a beautiful blur beneath us. I always feel safer with my brother than I do with anyone else.

I never planned to attend school in Colorado. I only applied so I could have an excuse to spend a little time with my brother, convincing my parents to fly me out here for this visit. I wasn't prepared to like it. In fact, I was certain I'd feel the opposite. But for miles along the highway there are only open fields and horses and so much sky. I feel excited, happy.

I am seventeen.

You can't really see Boulder until you come right up on it and then there it is. The snowy Flatirons fall into view, foothills spreading in either direction, the valley nestled below. We pull into the circular driveway in front of Regent Hall just in time for the information session for prospective students. He tells me what time he'll be waiting for me.

"You're not coming?"

"I've got an errand."

"Wish me luck?"

"You don't need any."

After the meeting, I wander through the Fine Arts building and try to envision myself there. Students work in small studios, their doors swung open and music playing. Most are painters or work in ceramics. A few make installations. I'm too timid to ask anybody questions even though I know I should. I find the photo lab. It's decent, certainly better than many, but all in all, the art department has very little compared to the other programs where I've been accepted. It doesn't matter. I can shoot anywhere. That's what I tell myself.

Patrick isn't waiting for me, but after a few minutes I see his motorcycle making the turn at the light. He doesn't ask me about the presentation, just hands me my helmet and gestures for me to climb on. We speed off, leaving the campus behind us. Patrick makes the turn up toward the Flatirons and we snake our way up the steep road passing boulders and jagged red rock faces amidst pines. I lean in to him, trying to talk, but my words blow back inside my helmet.

We hit ice, skidding into the other lane. I close my eyes. Wait for it. But nothing happens. We don't fly off a cliff or get hit by a car. I feel my brother's body vibrate, my arms wrapped round him, but I can't tell if he's shaking or laughing. When get to the lookout point, he turns the bike around to head back down, without even stopping for the view.

"Let's get a drink," he says. "Anyway, you were never one for tourist shots."

Back in town, we park near Pearl Street and walk for a block or so along the mall.

"Quinn's." Patrick points up at the sign. I've made friends with the bartender, so don't worry about ever getting carded."

He puts his arm around me and we walk inside. Two old men sit at a table playing chess and drinking coffee. Otherwise the place is empty, dark. An enormous moose is mounted and displayed on the wall, somehow still majestic with its sad spread of antlers, the unseeing eyes. We take our drinks and move to a table in the window. It's sunny outside but the light doesn't penetrate the glass.

Neither of us seems to know what to say.

"Tommy bought me a new camera," I tell him. "Two and a quarter."

"And how is our old man?"

"They know you got kicked out of school."

Patrick doesn't say anything.

"Why didn't you just tell them?"

"You know how they are—always needing a story to tell their friends."

"Maybe. I don't know."

"A few years without me and you've already bought into their bullshit."

"No," I tell him. "I mean, they love you. Us."

He gets up and walks toward the bathroom.

I shouldn't have brought it up. I should have let him bring it up.

The longer he's gone, the more anxious I become. I fiddle with his smokes, folding and unfolding the foil liner of the pack. I pull one out and light it. Patrick and I used to steal our mother's cigarettes, taking them down to the beach and hiding behind the jetty. We'd try to blow smoke rings. Or inhale without coughing. Usually we never finished a whole one, stubbing them out in the sand or watching the whirl of the tide carry them away.

I look up and Patrick is standing beside the table. It is the first time he has ever reminded me of our father. He grabs the cigarette out of my mouth and crushes it in the ashtray.

"Don't smoke."

"Trick? What's up?"

"Please," he says.

He covers his eyes with his sunglasses. I try to make him smile, tell him a story about orientation and all the other petrified would-be freshman in the auditorium, their parents asking how the different disciplines rank. He just stands there, finishing his drink.

I can barely hear him when he tells me, "Don't come to school here."

"What are you talking about?"

He shakes his head. "Nothing."

Shasta turns off Baseline Road to take me home. He knows I finagled my way out of the dorms at the end of last semester and moved off campus. Dark fields flank the long drive up into Chautauqua. We pass the turnoff for the lodge and the dining hall on our way to the cottages.

"Dude, you live in the park?" Kim says.

"Yes, but you've got to stop calling me dude."

"Sorry, dude." He cracks up.

We pull up under the cottonwood tree in front of my house and Shasta asks if they can see my place. And I think, it is always this way— me and the stoner boys. Just like Patrick and Spit and me in Spit's basement. All these guys probably have girlfriends, but here they are anyway. With me.

Kim flips through my albums, settling on Bowie. I still feel shaky from the bar. I don't really want them here. But inertia. I only have wine so I open it and fill four small juice glasses. Kim and Shasta knock theirs together and tilt them back, draining them. I pass one to Nick who is making me nervous by looking at my photographs. That's always the sign. If I care what someone thinks of my work. Kim spares me the embarrassment of saying anything stupid to Nick by grabbing my hand and making me dance. He ducks under the light fixture with every turn. When the song ends I sit on the floor, my back against the sofa.

"This surface is totally trés bien." Shasta taps the coke out onto the broken piece of granite I use for a table. "And by the way, if your living room is red, I can only imagine the boudoir."

"Keep imagining," I say.

"Look at this." Kim lifts up the phone. "It's all Dial M for Murder and shit." He glances at me to make sure it's okay, then dials. "Hey…with Shasta…No, at Quinn's…Anna?" He looks at us with genuine surprise. "Damn. She hung up."

"Never say you're at a chick's place. Especially not at three in the morning,"

"She was sleeping."

"One thing we're definitely not going to be doing." Shasta gestures to the lines he's carved out on the table. He removes the guts from a Bic pen and offers it to me. I snort one and instantly regret it. But that doesn't stop me from having a second. Nick declines, says he has to be at work early. He lights a cigarette and hands it to me then lights another for himself. We exchange a look that lasts a second too long.

"That shit will kill you." Shasta waves the smoke away from his face and we laugh.

By the time Kim picks up the phone again, Shasta says he can take a hint. We all walk outside onto my porch. Shasta could stand here chatting for another hour, but Kim urges him to come on.

"Nick?"

"I think I'll like the walk," Nick says.

"Merci for an excellent evening then." Shasta kisses my cheek.

"Wait." I go back inside and find the rest of the coke in my bag. I hand Shasta the vial and tell him it's on the house. He protests, but only for a moment. All I know is I don't want it anywhere near me.

Nick and I sit on the steps in the cold and the near-dawn light. There are still a few stars. I can't recall if there was ever a moon. Alone with him in the quiet, I feel shy in a way I'd never feel with the others. He tells me he'd like to have one of my photographs. I ask which, so I can make him a print.

"You choose."

"Shasta told me you're a carpenter."

"I had to leave school. Trying to save enough money to go back."

I like that he's not embarrassed about it.

He describes the house he's helping build up in Sunshine

"I bike up there sometimes."

"I've seen you, actually," he says. "Not up the canyon, but in town. With your camera slung over your back."

I'm struggling to come up with something to say. Not because I'm bored. I'm anything but bored. I just don't want to sound all amped up, twitchy. Nick just looks at me. The silence doesn't seem to make him uncomfortable. I shift around on the stoop, wishing for my cigarettes, so I'd have something to do with my hands.

"What were we talking about? Building houses?"

"Sort of," he says, "but the truth is I'd like to kiss you and if I don't just say so, I'll sit here talking about nothing to keep you from kicking me out."

"I'm not kicking you out. You can kiss me if you want."

He pulls me closer and presses his warm lips on my forehead then wraps his arm around me, traces his lips soft along my neck.

"There," he says, holding me against him.

I haven't even kissed him on the mouth, but I feel like something has happened. I think about the guys I've slept with. How I never bring them back here so I can leave before they wake. How I rarely give out my phone number and always regret when I do.

I take his hand and pull him through the doorway, close the door behind us and lead him down the narrow hallway to my room.

"It's blue—don't tell Shasta."

"Almost purple," he says.

At first, I'm not even sure what day it is. Saturday? When I muster the courage to peek outside the sun is dropping behind the mountains. This close to the trailhead, my cottage is quickly swallowed in shadow. But I don't mind the dark coming on. I feel as if I've been balancing bricks on my forehead. The drinks. The lines. The cigarettes.

Don't, I tell myself. Don't count.

I have this terrible habit of always trying to add it all up. I decide to forget all that. But the detritus in the living room reminds me. Dried red wine stains along the rims of the glasses. Rolling papers and Shasta's dead Bic. The ashtray. The worst part is the flicker of a thought that if I hadn't given away the coke, I'd do just a little bit of it. Only to get myself going. Maybe that's why Patrick always cleans everything up before he goes to bed.

I ring my brother, but he doesn't answer. At this point, it is already Saturday night. I'll try to catch him tomorrow before Nadine forces him to take her out for mimosas. I prop the door open to air out my house. It feels much colder than it had last night. I put all the albums away and clear off the table. After I wash all the glasses, I make myself a cup of tea. I try not to think about Nick. I don't want to get caught up in it. In him. Before long, I crawl back in bed.

In the morning, there is snow. A lot of snow. Dusting the Flatirons. Hanging heavy on the branches of trees. And there is also Nick—standing on my front porch, the Sunday paper and a bag of groceries in his arms, like some sort of apparition. An old white Scout parked in the snow on the road behind him.

"I'm glad we didn't sleep together," I say.

A couple weeks pass before I get nervous about not being able to reach Patrick. Knowing him, he's skiing. I picture the two of us taking lessons on the icy trails at Devil's Head in Wisconsin. Figuring out how it wasn't so different from ice-skating and the way you use your edges to make turns. He used to tease me when I'd get frightened on the lift because it seemed unnatural to be looking down on the tops of trees. Blue-green pines muscling their way up out of the snow in search of sky. Eventually I got the hang of it and looked forward to those long days on the slopes. But I think we both always preferred the sea.

I continue to call Patrick, but I never reach him. Or even Scotty. I'll admit Nick is a bit of a distraction. But it's also the end of term and I'm often away from home, studying or making prints for my final portfolio. I convince myself he's been calling while I'm on campus in the darkroom or taking exams.

It is Nick who finally offers to drive me down to see him.

"Or take my car, if you don't want to wait until I can bring you."

"Maybe he just needs space."

"Quinn," he says. "Go find your brother."

I'm nervous the whole way to Denver. In part because I've lost the habit of driving. Mostly I'm worried. I don't know why exactly. Nothing is wrong. We haven't had an argument. I would have gotten a call if something terrible had happened to him. Right? But why haven't I heard from him?

I park in front of Scotty's house, go up to the porch, and ring the bell. Nobody's there. Bix barks and barks. He climbs on the back of the couch and pokes his snout between the blinds, nosing the window and leaving slobber marks on the glass. I try to calm him, but he just barks louder. I push my sunglasses up on my head and attempt to peer inside, but I can't really see anything. I look for Patrick's key in its hiding spot under a withered houseplant in a terracotta pot. Nothing. I could sit on the steps and wait, but Bix is going ballistic. Poor dog. I write a note and prop it between the storm and the door. I don't drop it through the metal letterbox because I don't want Bix to eat it.

My sense of direction can sometimes fail me, but I find my way back to Mandy's. The sad sight of his sofa and the lawn that is more dirt than grass cheers me a bit. The door opens just enough for Mandy's mouth and beard to appear above the chain. He tells me he'll be right back. He closes the door and is gone for a few minutes. I perch on the arm of the sofa looking out at the street as if Patrick will pull up any time now.

Mandy steps out, holding the door so I can't see inside, then shuts it behind him. It feels out of context to see him in the fresh air and sunlight. I ask if he's seen Patrick.

"Damn, Little Sister." He doesn't look at me, but past me. "Didn't he tell you?"

"Tell me?"

Mandy seems uncomfortable.

"He's in L.A. He moved out there."

I turn away from him toward the walkway in his front yard, clumps of dirty snow still lingering at the curb. The storm must have killed his forsythia. The branches are bare again, the yellow petals scattered beneath the shrub, anemic and rotting.

"Hermosa Beach," he says. "Actually, I'm not really sure which town." Like he's trying to make me feel better about being the last to know. Or like he just remembered he wasn't supposed to say anything.

It seems impossible. I cry the whole way back to Boulder. I cry so hard that at one point, I have to pull Nick's Scout over on the narrow shoulder, cars passing and passing. I finish my last cigarette then sift through his glove box finding only a crumpled pack with nothing in it.

I walk down the steps of school, looking for Patrick amidst the bell ringing and the confusion of the schoolyard. All the kids from different grades pour out of various entrances, boarding buses or car-pooling home. Some parents chat in clusters on the sidewalk or call out to their children. I wait, high up on the steps, so he can see me. But he never shows up. One by one everyone else disappears.

After a little while, I walk around the school to make sure I haven't missed him. I see my teacher, Miss Patterson of the long blonde ponytail and print dresses whom, like all the other second-graders, I adore. She's holding a stack of folders and walking to her car, but she doesn't notice me. I sit on the ground, my back against the fence, watching a couple of older boys shooting hoops, playing a game of H.O.R.S.E., but pretty soon they get ready to leave, too. They stop in front of me, their shadows blocking the sun as I look up at them.

The one holding the basketball kneels down. "You're Patrick's sister, right?"

"He got in trouble," the other one says. "They sent him home."

"Oh," I say. "Okay." I watch them walk away, passing the ball between them.

I get up and walk along the perimeter of the basketball court toward the gate. I run my fingers along the chinks of chain-link fence until I come to a section covered in milkweed that has sprung up out of a crack in the asphalt. Tangled vines climbing higher than I can reach. I stop to look at the little pods that have yet to open, only when I brush the leaves aside, what I see isn't a nascent flower, but a kind of cocoon, translucent green and furled into a tight bundle. I can see the outline of the butterfly already. The way its wings fold in on themselves, and even the stripes described on the wings beneath the thin membrane. A monarch. The chrysalis dangles there, camouflaged among the leaves, like a secret I have to keep. And I do keep it.

I walk home thinking about the butterfly in the pupa waiting to molt, how fragile it seems, protected by only a thin layer of skin and a handful of leaves. I forget that my family has neglected to pick me up. I even forget to worry about whatever my brother might have done or how much trouble he's gotten into. All I can think about is that little life waiting to break free.

I take the long way home instead of cutting through the park. When I open the back door, my mother is standing in the kitchen with my father. They turn around and look at me.

"Oh, honey," she says. "I'm sorry."

"She's fine—look at her. You're a big girl now, aren't you, Quinn?" my father says.

During recess or after school, I make sure nobody else sees what I am doing and I find an excuse to visit my butterfly. Each day I watch its progression, noticing even the smallest changes in the shape or smoothness of the chrysalis. Hoping maybe just maybe, I will catch the monarch emerging like a flame. But one afternoon, there is only an empty opaque shell drooping from the vine, the pale skin of the pupa ruptured and rumpled like a miniature paper lantern battered by the wind.

"Good," I say. "You got out."

But then I cry.

When I get back to Boulder, I return Nick's truck and thank him. Then I tell him I don't want to see him anymore.

He says he doesn't understand.

"I don't deserve you."

"What are you talking about?"

"Anyway, I'm transferring schools." I had not known this until now, but I realize that both of the things I've told him are true.

Nick tries to console me, but he doesn't try to change my mind. He is, in fact, entirely decent about all of it. He doesn't try to spoon-feed me platitudes or say things like, "It's only California." And he doesn't try to convince me that as soon as my brother has a phone installed he'll call me and we will sort it all out. He's never even met Patrick, and somehow he knows him better than I do.

That night, I go out and I get good and drunk at Quinn's, the only bar I can get into without an ID. I pick up a frat boy whose name I won't remember. I snort lines with him in the bathroom before we end up fucking in the cramped backseat of his 320i, parked at the far west end of Pearl.

Afterward, I bike home, climbing the long steady slope of 9th Street in the dark. I sit on the cold steps of my cottage until first light when a deer streaks across the open meadow. Fast and lightfooted and solitary.

When summer comes, I move back east. Back to our beach house by the sea. My parents rarely return from Chicago to use it, but they could never bring themselves to sell it. I feel safe here even though it erodes more and more each year, our small stretch of beachfront all but disappearing. But for now it's still here, up on tall stilts, casting shadows over the fine white sand and dunes. The beach grass gone silver in the sun. The Atlantic as cold and gray as it always was.

Late one night the phone rings, waking me from the kind of deep dreaming that happens when you are lulled by the waves. There is no voice on the other end. But I swear I can hear him breathing. Inhaling and exhaling smoke. I stand by the window in the dark, looping the telephone cord around my fingers and staring out at the dark line of the sea.

I continue making photographs. With images I can tell the story the way I want it to be. Nobody else knows how it was before; only Patrick knows. Whenever a shadow passes in front of my viewfinder, I hope it is my brother, coming up out of the dunes to find me, just as he always used to.

But he's never there.

It's early autumn when the monarchs come. And neither of us can believe it. First, a single monarch alights on the windowsill. Graceful flick of its wings. Then another perches beside it, near Patrick's hand. When we look outside, the pair of chestnut trees in our backyard is aflame. Branches thrumming with thousands of small orange and black wings. The sky is filled with monarchs. A kaleidoscope.

We run outside amidst the commotion of wings and stand between the enormous trees, the boughs stretching high over our heads, the green canopy of leaves transformed to the color of sunset. Monarchs fly and float, swirling everywhere around us. The butterflies land on our outstretched arms and on our shoulders, even in our hair. So light you can barely feel them, but you can hear them. The air vibrates with the fluttering of wings, like so many fragile decks of cards being shuffled.

One lands on my wrist and I watch as it crawls toward my palm.

"There you are," I say, knowing it was meant for me. After finding the chrysalis in the schoolyard, I'd asked the librarian for a book that had everything to do with butterflies, especially monarchs. "They're migrating," I tell him. "To Mexico."

"Right," Patrick says.

"No, really. That's what they do. They overwinter."

"Wish we could go, too."

"I know."

I stare at him, barefooted, the damp dark grass beneath his bony, veiny feet. Still tan from last summer. His pale green eyes surrounded by dark lashes. His laugh when a butterfly lands on his head then takes flight again. Monarchs clutter and cull along his arms, undulating. Tiny flames lapping at his collar close to his blonde curls.

We don't call out for anyone else to come and witness this great flight.

We stand together, as quiet as we can, inviting stillness. Inviting grace. We both understand this is something we'll never see again. But the once is everything.

I do not lift my camera from its strap around my neck. I do not make a picture.

Not of the butterflies.

And not of my brother.

I don't need to.

Neither of us will ever tell anybody else about it. Not the way the trees had come alive, inhaling black and exhaling orange as the monarchs close and open their wings. Not the way the butterflies feel landing on our skin. The way they glow and glimmer with the last of the light.

I hold my monarch, still cupped in my fingers. All the others have drifted up and away, finding different paths to the trees, gathering there for warmth. I open my palm and the butterfly flickers between us before taking flight. Patrick reaches out and takes my other hand. We look at each other knowing what we both know, lit up with the excitement of knowing it.

Acknowledgments

Very likely this book would not exist without Lucia Berlin, whose friendship and mentorship rescued and reoriented me more than once. Thanks to my mother and fellow traveler Joan Geoghegan, my brother Barry who taught me a thing or two, and my sister Chris, forever my inspiration, my guru, my guide. Thanks must also go to the memory of my inimitable father, a storyteller himself. A mountain of gratitude belongs to Karen Auvinen with whom I've long shared this writing journey. There are not enough ways to thank Lovisa Stephenson for her indomitable belief in me and these stories. Grazie infinite to Diana Mastrodomenico for her exquisite editorial eye, and so much else. Special thanks to Jeannette Montgomery Barron whose photograph graces the cover of this collection and captures its many moods. Several Rome-based writers generously bestowed their comradeship and wisdom along the way, among them Jahan Khajavi, Francesca Marciano, Chiara Barzini, Giancarlo DiTrapano, Andrea di Robilant, George Minot, Allison Grimaldi-Donahue, Elizabeth Farren, and Carlos Dews—thank you. Many others supported my writing or have been there for me in other untold ways: thanks to Ted Kruckel, Christine Finley, Michelle Rogers, Martin Holvoet, Team Chicago (you know who you are), Susan Bradley Smith, Michael Carroll, Steve Emerson, Jenny Dorn, Reg Saner, Rhonda Claridge, Staci Haynes, Dave Cullen, Erika Krouse, Heidi Pitlor, Amanda Holmes, Rachel Donadio, Joan Geller, Sarah Morgan, Paula Derrow, Sophy Downes, Sarah Wetzel, Anita Ross, Tara Keenan, Lauren Sunstein, Shannon Russell, Dolen Perkins-Valdez, Karin Dorell, Susana Cavallo, Kim Connor, and Mark Bosco. Finally, thank you to Andrew Gifford and the Santa Fe Writers Project.

About the Author

Photo: Lovisa Stephenson

Elizabeth Geoghegan was born in New York, grew up in the Midwest, and lives in Rome. She is the author of *Natural Disasters* and the bestselling memoir *The Marco Chronicles*. Her work has appeared in *The Paris Review*, *The Best Travel Writing*, *El Pais*, *Words Without Borders*, and elsewhere.

The author can be found on Instagram @elizabeth_geoghegan

Also from Santa Fe Writers Project

If the Ice Had Held by Wendy J. Fox

Melanie Henderson's life is a lie. The scandal of her birth and the identity of her true parents is kept from her family's small, conservative Colorado town. Not even she knows the truth: that her birth mother was just 14 and unmarried to her father, a local boy who drowned when he tried to take a shortcut across an icy river.

"Razor-sharp...written with incredible grace and assurance."
— Benjamin Percy, author of *The Dark Net*

Patagonian Road: A Year Alone Through Latin America by Kate McCahill

Patagonian Road chronicles Kate McCahill's solo journey from Guatemala to Argentina. In her struggles with language, romance, culture, service, and homesickness, she personifies a growing culture of women for whom travel is not a path to love but to meaningful work, rare inspiration, and profound self-discovery.

"This welcome (and timely) call to explore foreign borders as well as our own comfort zones is highly recommended."
— *Library Journal*

Bystanders by Tara Laskowski

"'Short story' and 'thriller' tend to be incompatible genres, but not in the hands of Tara Laskowski. BYSTANDERS is a bold, riveting mash-up of Hitchcockian suspense and campfire-tale chills."
— Jennifer Egan, author of *A Visit from the Goon Squad* and *The Keep*

About Santa Fe Writers Project

SFWP is an independent press founded in 1998 that embraces a mission of artistic preservation, recognizing exciting new authors, and bringing out of print work back to the shelves.

Find us on Facebook, Twitter @sfwp, and at www.sfwp.com $\int fwp$)